After the Last Post

A Selection of Further Titles by Brenda McBryde

Fiction

HANNAH ROBSON
HANNAH'S DAUGHTER

THE DANDELION CLOCK *

* available from Severn House

After the
Last Post

Brenda McBryde

This first world edition published in Great Britain 2003 by
SEVERN HOUSE PUBLISHERS LTD of
9–15 High Street, Sutton, Surrey SM1 1DF.
This first world edition published in the USA 2003 by
SEVERN HOUSE PUBLISHERS INC of
595 Madison Avenue, New York, N.Y. 10022.

British Library Cataloguing in Publication Data

McBryde, Brenda, 1918-
   After the last post
   1.   British - Australia - Fiction
   2.   England - Social life and customs - 1945- - Fiction
   3.   Australia - Social life and customs - Fiction
   I.   Title
   823.9'14 [F]

ISBN 0-7278-5942-0

Typeset by Palimpsest Book Production Ltd.,
Polmont, Stirlingshire, Scotland.
Printed and bound in Great Britain by
MPG Books Ltd., Bodmin, Cornwall.

Foreword

In the opening chapters of *The Dandelion Clock*, the book which precedes this one, a group of friends in Eastport, a major port in the north-east of England, are at the start of their careers. These are the carefree days in the 1930s before the outbreak of the Second World War. These young men and their girl friends go around together meeting in cafes in the rain, picnics on fine days, full of ideals and argument. They are in love with George Gershwin's music and pretty fox-trotting girls and they bang around the Northumbrian countryside in clapped-out Morris Oxfords and ancient Bentleys, dreaming up brilliant futures for themselves.

These were to undergo a drastic revision when war broke out. The office desk and the university would be put on hold to allow students and apprentices and budding salesmen to serve king and country in the cause of freedom from tyranny.

Within their group, a close network of friendships had grown up, some dating from schooldays, though their standards of living and consequent views were diverse. Simon Poole was the star of the local rugby team but earned a living as an uninspired insurance clerk. Quentin, much indulged only child of rich parents, was the heavy intellectual. Handsome Alec Cruddas, pulsing with drama, was well placed as junior reporter on the *Northern Echo*. Eric, bank clerk, a timid chap but solid friend for rough-and-ready Jacky, who worked as teaboy in an estate agency and wore

1

a black dog on his shoulder. Colin Rankin was a sober Scot with a finely tuned sense of duty and responsibility in one so young; and, lately come to join the group, Andrew Mount, a trainee doctor.

As for the girls in the company, Cathy and Norah were training as nurses and Evie was a pupil teacher. Other girls, whose presence is not so relevant to this plot, joined the women's services once war was declared. There was another girl, an outsider from choice. Hilde Mullerman, a refugee from Hitler's pogrom against the Jews, was a student nurse along with Cathy and Norah at the hospital where Andrew was studying medicine. Andrew fell in love with her and went on loving her till the end of his days.

Like most people in Britain, they were unaware that the country was under imminent threat from Germany. It had been a bit of a lark to join the Territorials, a week's annual camp in moth-eaten bell tents, instruction on how to march, clean a rifle and dig a latrine, but they were unaware that the country was poised at the edge of a crater.

Men with foresight who warned of Hitler's territorial appetite were scorned as warmongers. Not until Europe was ablaze did the nation see that Hitler must be stopped. Not unexpectedly, an ultimatum by Britain and France was rejected by Hitler and war was officially declared, on 3rd September, by France and Britain against Germany.

Simon was the first to enlist, followed by the others. Colin put aside his law books, reluctantly, 'for the duration'. The drill halls throughout Britain filled with would-be soldiers, sailors and airmen to be measured for uniforms of navy blue, khaki or air-force blue, all Joe Bloggs, the chef, the plumber, solicitor, postman, poet. As the cream rose to the surface stripes were handed out. Then it was time to go to France.

Andrew, now a lieutenant in the Royal Army Medical Corps, stayed behind to look after the wounded on the beach at Dunkirk and spent the next five years in a German prisoner of war camp. Those who came back from Dunkirk were sent again to other places, other battles and dangers in far-off lands for the next five years.

During that time the special group of friends was scattered. Some did not survive. The sea, Quentin's chosen element, claimed him when a torpedo struck his ship. Jacky trod on a mine in the North African desert and Colin's landmine blew up before he could defuse it. Cathy and Norah were out where the action was, seeing at first hand what a mortar shell can do to a young man's body. Alec, the beautiful, was scarred for life when his Spitfire caught fire over Kent during the Battle of Britain. Simon battled on, wounded, repaired and ready to fight again, but was denied his prize at the end of the war. Cathy, his sweetheart from childhood, married somebody else. Andrew's release from prison camp brought little of the hoped for happiness. Yes. It is a sad tale in parts. But war is sad.

Victory came, shamefacedly bearing wreaths, and the survivors of that early company of friends, older, wiser, came together again to remember old times and absent friends.

As for Norah, what happened to her is described in this present piece of writing.

Part One

One

1949, almost four years since the Second World War was dragged, kicking and screaming to a close and Britain, impoverished by her immense war effort, was laid low like a winded boxer. The nation that was once intoxicated with victory had waited in vain for the promised good times. They were still to come. Everything in England from industrial goods to food imports was in short supply. No paint for shabby buildings. No glass for broken windows. No money. In so many homes, no wage-earner left.

But at least, the fighting is over. Cathy Webster clung to this thought. The images of war must go, of convoys of ambulances rocking over the North African desert, trundling through the mud of Normandy; of stretcher bearers stumbling into medical posts, laying down their burdens wherever they could find space. *Hitler is dead*, she reminded herself. *We can put all the bad times behind us. I live in a country which has won its freedom and I am married to the most wonderful man in the world.*

He was balancing one foot on the kitchen stool, giving his shoes a final polish before leaving to catch the 0800 train to London. He looked across at his dreaming wife as she sat amongst the breakfast things, a letter still unopened in her hand. 'Aren't you going to open it then?'

She smiled fondly at him and slit the envelope with the bread knife. 'It's from Norah. I like to linger over the anticipation, like saving the marzipan on the Christmas

7

cake.' She withdrew the page of neat writing. 'Good heavens!'

Ray Webster, with a glance at his watch, put the shoe-cleaning kit away. 'What's up?'

'She's off to Australia.'

'That's a bit sudden. Does she know anyone there?'

'Remember I told you about that Australian soldier who fell for her in a big way?'

'I thought he was killed in New Guinea.'

'He was but his sister has invited Norah to visit. All expenses paid!'

'Gee, she's lucky.' He drained his teacup. 'Got to go, dear. Tell me the rest tonight.' He bent to kiss her cheek.

'She's sailing from Liverpool on 14 February, on the *Himalaya.* Oh, Ray dear, can we go and see her off? '

'Bit difficult for me to take the day off, darling. Lot of chaps are after my job. And I wouldn't be happy for you to go on your own.'

'She'll be so miserable if none of her friends are there to see her off.'

'Tell you what, I'll drop a note to Andy. His practice is not far from Liverpool. He'll go. Really must be off, darling.'

The man who had served in the Second World War as an officer in the Coldstream Guards reached for his bowler hat and umbrella. No sign now of the tuberculosis which had plucked him from active service and sent him into a sanatorium. He made his way past an ironing board and a clothes basket.

'Don't forget to drink your milk and your orange juice.' He gave her a cheeky grin. 'You're a precious vessel now.'

Cathy and Norah had been inseparable friends since schooldays. During the war they had served overseas as army nurses. Nothing came between them until the peace was won and Cathy got married.

'This won't make any difference between us,' Cathy had whispered to Norah as she left for her honeymoon. 'Ray will be just like a brother to you when you get to know him better.'

That hadn't worked. Norah knew it wouldn't. 'Two's company. Three's none.' For her to have sprung news of her trip to Australia in this way was a measure of the distance which had grown between them.

Ray Webster was already stepping out smartly for the station. Cathy had the day to herself. She cleared a space on the breakfast table. 'I'll write straightaway. When she hears she's going to be a godmother that'll cheer her up.'

Norah's parents also were taken by surprise by their daughter's decision to visit Australia. 'And where do these people live, that you are going to stay with?' her mother wanted to know.

'They have a farm somewhere in the north west of New South Wales near a place called Dog Creek.'

'Dog Creek! What kind of address is that, for goodness' sake?'

'If they're farmers, they'll be decent folk, Edith,' her husband assured her. 'Cattle, is it? Or sheep.'

'A bit of both, I think,' Norah said. 'And Marian, the daughter who's about my age, she breeds horses.'

'I reckon you'll have the time of your life, lass. Enjoy it.' Joe Moffat's reassurance was intended to erase the look of doubt in his wife's eye but after their daughter had left them to return to the hospital where she worked, the couple sat awhile in silence in the sunny front room of their terrace house, gamely trying to rationalize the wisps of worry she left behind.

'Lately, she seems so out of sorts with herself.'

'Like she's lost her rudder,' her father agreed. 'Should

9

never have married that jumped-up pip-squeak sea squab. Knocked her off course, he did.'

'Well maybe this trip will put the roses back in her cheeks.' His wife was fast returning to her customary common sense. 'Then she'll come back and settle down.'

Norah had not been able to hide her dismay at Cathy's marriage.

'No big thing,' her fellow nurses teased her. 'Girls do get married.'

But she was devastated. It was Cathy's choice of husband which riled Norah more than anything else. Like most of their friends, Norah had expected Cathy to marry Simon Poole, one of the group who went about together in the heady days of 1938 before thoughts of war intervened to change the direction of their lives. Fox-trotting to Henry Hall's dance band, holding hands in the back row of the cinema on Friday night, racketting along country roads in someone's broken-down Morris Cowley. Falling in love. The first of the boys to join the Territorials in the 1938 Munich crisis was Simon Poole, rugby full-back, insurance clerk, who had been in love with Cathy since schooldays.

Not all of those pre-war friendships survived. Simon's devotion to Cathy, however, never faltered. When he sought her out at the end of hostilities it was to learn that she was to marry someone else, an ex-patient of hers. He had fought a hard war in many campaigns and had been seriously wounded at the evacuation of Dunkirk, yet no wound could match the pain of losing Cathy.

Norah was as surprised and dismayed at Cathy's choice as the rest of her friends. She would have been so easy with Simon as Cathy's husband, but Ray Webster was an outsider. He whisked her away to live in the south of England and Simon transferred to the regular army then in administration of post-war German affairs.

Norah was desperately lonely but she admitted later she must have taken temporary leave of her senses when, in a fit of pique at what she regarded as a betrayal by Cathy, she married a man she had met in Italy during the war. Naval officer Peter Collins had pulled Norah from the sea when the ship she was serving in was sunk. It was a shaky foundation on which to build a marriage. The whole affair was a disaster and she sought a divorce immediately.

People were sorry for her, believing her to have been deserted after so brief a marriage and she did not disillusion them. Then, in 1948, when her spirits were at an all-time low, an invitation to visit Australia arrived, offering a chance to escape from gossipping tongues in the Sisters' Mess.

Dear Norah,
  I hope I may call you that since you were so nearly a member of our family.

Norah's eyes flew to the signature. 'Marian Reed' conveyed nothing.

You are the girl my brother Keith hoped to marry. He would have brought you here as his bride had he survived. Please come.

Captain Keith Russell, of the first volunteer Australian force to sail from Sydney on the *Queen Mary* at the start of hostilities in 1940, had been a frequent visitor to the military hospital in Egypt where Norah and Cathy were working in 1941. Tall, bronzed, a striking figure in his definitive slouch hat, he had escorted her around Cairo while he was based in Egypt. He was charming and entertaining and, when nothing more than friendship was demanded of her, Norah enjoyed his company.

The relationship took a dive, however, when, in 1942,

11

on the eve of his division's departure to repel the Japanese invasion of New Guinea, he asked her to marry him. For her this was a step too far. The letter in which she declined his proposal never reached him, however, and was eventually returned to her, unopened, stamped 'DECEASED'.

He never knew that she had turned him down nor did his family. They only knew that she was the girl he wanted to marry and this was enough to prompt them to send the invitation to visit.

She turned to the letter once more.

> Now that the shipping lines are resuming their Australian routes we would so much like to meet you. You will help my mother and father come to terms with the loss of their son and me with losing the best brother a girl ever had. I enclose a warrant for your expenses according to Keith's last wishes. I can meet you in Sydney whenever your ship comes in.

She was being offered a wonderful opportunity to get out of England for a while, to start her life anew without Cathy but how would these kind people react to the fact that she had never intended to marry their son? It seemed she must turn down their offer. Keith had been a good friend and a brave soldier. She would write straight away and explain that marriage had never been an option.

She began, *Dear Marian*, and got no further.

Was it out of the question to conceal the truth of her relationship with her brother? What would Cathy do in this situation? Cathy had liked Keith, had encouraged her to accept his proposal, couldn't understand why she turned him down, but it was no good. She knew she was different from other girls in that she did not want a husband, no matter how attractive. Would it be such a terrible thing to gloss over all that? After all, Keith himself had asked her to visit his homeland without him if he did not survive.

His words returned to her. One magical Egyptian evening he had said to her, 'If my number comes up, promise me you will go to see my homeland, meet my family and see what I am fighting for.'

Walking in the garden of the Cairo Club that perfumed evening it had not seemed to be a difficult promise to make. But that was before the game changed its name from friendship to something else.

Dear Marian.

The SS *Himalaya* was preparing to sail from the port of Liverpool with a full complement of passengers. Norah stood with the other passengers at the ship's rail but was not one of them. Her aloneness set her apart from the happy leavetaking around her.

The gangway was up. The crew handled the hawsers and made ready to sail. The mothering tugs took up position. Last farewells from the crowd on the quayside were drowned in a triumphant blast from the ship's funnel. Sedately she moved into the pool of the Mersey to begin her long voyage to Australia, where the sun shone all the time, where meat and butter and clothing were unrationed, where you could pick a lemon from a tree and bask on the beach till you fried. Where no one knew Norah Collins's secret.

As the strip of water between the ship and the land widened, she lifted a hand in a poignant gesture of farewell to someone in the crowd below and the man who had come to see her off lifted his trilby in solemn salute.

He did not wait to see the last of the ship. Farewells to ships were excruciatingly long-drawn-out and he knew that Norah would feel the same. He wished her well. He wished her joy of this very untypical leap into the unknown. Setting his hat firmly on his head against the brisk sea

13

breeze he made for the car park, pushing his way through families suddenly subdued and breaking apart, thinking their thoughts.

Norah turned away. 'Poor Andrew.'

Dr Andrew Mount was thirty-three years old although he sometimes felt that he had already lived a lifetime. His appearance bore this out. His gait was stooped, his shoulders hunched. He rarely lifted his eyes from the pavement in front of him. He was remembering Norah as she was when he first met her, before the war, before chaos. 'The snow queen in her ivory tower' the others called her, Simon, Alec and the rest.

Resolutely he put away memories of those carefree pre-war days when young men could dream of a bright future, when ideals and ambitions fuelled the planning of great enterprises. Such thoughts did him no good. They were hardly credible now and merely reawakened the contempt he felt for himself.

He climbed into his Morris Minor and lit a cigarette, reflecting that, by getting away from the clutter of might-have-beens to a place where she was not known, Norah had boldly grasped the nettle and was to be admired for that. He put his foot down hard on the accelerator. It would be dark before he reached Ambleside.

As that February day faded into a chilly evening, Norah and a few passengers hung about on the deck of the *Himalaya* to catch a final glimpse of the Liver Birds of Liverpool. The pilot, his responsibility at an end, climbed down the rope ladder into the harbour launch and was borne back to the land and his tea. The ship's captain took over the bridge once more and the heavy-laden ship, so cumbersome in port, so graceful at sea, gathered up her power and swung confidently out of the Mersey estuary and into the Irish Sea, leaving a wake of garbage in a sea that was the colour of dirty drains.

A mean wind promised rain. Norah Collins pulled her coat close and went below to her cabin to unpack. There was no going back now. She was on her way, fretted by doubts but none the less resolute to make the visit worthwhile for the family of Captain Keith Russell MC.

She washed and changed into a pretty dress and added a string of small pearls. Her blonde hair, dampened by the sea mist, fell into soft waves at the nape of her neck. As the gong sounded for dinner, she braced herself to meet strangers who would share her table. Fellow passengers looked up as she entered the dining saloon and wondered who was this good-looking young woman travelling alone.

Two

S everal of the passengers on board the *Himalaya* were
Australians. Caught on the wrong side of the world
when war broke out in 1939, they had joined the British
armed forces and were now heading for home with stories
to tell that would earn many a free beer in the pubs 'back o'
the black stump'. Right from the start there was a sense of
easy companionship on board and an exchange of wartime
anecdotes, but Norah had already acquired the name of
being a bit of a loner and did not join in with her own
experiences.

She was one of the few passengers to venture on deck
during the bad weather in the Bay of Biscay. Choppy seas
and a sharp wind kept most of them below deck. To her, the
buffetting acted as a counter-irritant for her troubled mind.
Holding her face to the salt wind she thought, let it hurt.
Let it sting. '*Blow, blow thou winter wind, thou art not so
unkind,*' came to her mind, 'as someone I could mention.'

It took a bold Australian to break into the bleak reserve
of the well-wrapped figure butting into the wind. 'Mind if
I join you?'

Without waiting for a reply, he fell into step beside her.
'Most of the passengers are flat out on their bunks, very
sorry for themselves. You must be made of sterner stuff.'

Although his manner was quite inoffensive Norah would
have preferred to be alone, to reflect upon the turn of events
which had led to her taking this quite extraordinary step of

16

travelling alone to Australia to stay with people she had never met. But the young man was studying her face, seeming to expect some kind of response.

'I learned to overcome sea-sickness during the war,' she said. 'I had a job to do and it had priority.'

He grinned. 'A sailor, perhaps?'

'In a way. I was a nurse on a hospital ship.'

He was obviously impressed but Norah, adept in the art of polite discouragement and the deflecting of curiosity about her personal affairs, encouraged him to talk about himself. He had driven tanks in the desert under Wavell's command.

'A real bonza general. Didn't get a fair crack of the whip.'

If he'd known that she, too, had served in the desert he would have gone on talking for hours.

The days grew warmer after they passed Cape Finistère. Softer airs swept the ship. Passengers emerged from their cabins and looked for nooks where their deck chairs would be out of the wind. The young men sought out Norah for a partner in deck quoits and table tennis. Whether she wished it or not she was being drawn into the ship's daily round.

The grey seas took on a bluer tone as lowering northern skies gave way to a brilliant infinity. Cotton-wool clouds sailed serenely over the ship as she made for the Canary Islands and Norah's low spirits seeped away in the company of determinedly friendly passengers.

There was a marked change in the reserved young woman who embarked at Liverpool. On board the *Himalaya* her world was ordered for her, no decisions were required of her beyond the choice between her two dresses that were suitable to wear for the evening meal. Sunshine and sea air promoted in her a feeling of wellbeing. She pushed to the back of her mind the ordeal she must face on reaching

Sydney. That was six weeks away. She could enjoy six weeks of relaxation.

After rounding the Cape they entered the Indian Ocean where they parted company from tankers making for the oil fields of the Middle East and followed their own lonely course across the Southern Ocean attended only by circling albatrosses. No other ships were in sight on this little-used sea lane apart from the occasional glimpse of a Japanese tuna-fishing boat. Peace of mind such as Norah had not experienced for some time encapsulated her as the ship swung along towards the striated cliffs of South Australia. When the ship entered Sydney's spectacular harbour her wonder equalled that of all on board.

'You beaut!' the young men greeted their homeland with delight. 'Here I come!'

The bows of the *Himalaya* cut a swathe through jewelled water. Creeks and inlets nibbled at the wandering inner shoreline of the vast harbour. Flowering trees and green lawns surrounding stately colonial residences crept right to the water's edge. Like a shoal of sharp white handkerchiefs small sailing boats crewed by cheeky schoolboys scudded across the path of sea-going liners in a racy game of 'chicken', driving the demented pilots to fury. The air, the sky, the leaping prow of the ship threw off streaks of spangled light to dazzle the eye on this brilliant Saturday afternoon in March. It seemed to Norah that all the superlatives used by the Australians to describe their harbour were entirely justified. Excitedly the landmarks were pointed out to 'new chums' like Norah; the Sailors' Chapel on the South Head, a marker for mariners, Mrs MacQuarrie's Chair, a spit of land inside the harbour where the wife of an early governor used to sit among the oleanders to bid farewell to his ship on every voyage he undertook and the little island in the very middle of the harbour called Pinchguts for good reason by the convicts who had once been imprisoned there.

A vision of the red noses and chilblains she had left behind in England came to Norah's mind; of grey skies and figures wrapped in mufflers. In Australia on such a Saturday as this the beach and the surf called. It was a day for picnics and barbecues, to be up and about in energetic sport of one kind or another A day to be young. What, thought Norah, do they do with their old folk?

Sidling cannily to her berth at Pyrmont docks, the *Himalaya* shut down her engines and announced her arrival with a final blast from her funnel.

The gangway clattered down. 'God's own country!' the Aussies sang out. 'We're back!' to the welcoming parties on the dock.

As the scuffle with luggage began, Norah's heart beat a little faster. The fun bit was over. Her trial was about to begin. She must act like the prospective daughter-in-law Keith's family took her to be. Recalling her affection for him was not difficult. They had shared a happy companionship until he pressed too far. She hoped that his family would not ask too many direct questions, for she would not be persuaded into telling lies if she could avoid it.

Marian Reed identified without difficulty the woman she had come to meet. Of all the bustling noisy passengers preparing to land, one stood hesitant, anxiously surveying the crowd below. She was tall and slim and beautiful, her blonde hair folded in a neat French pleat. Amongst the crumpled shirts and shorts of those around her, her simple dress had a certain elegance. She was Keith's girl for sure.

Norah was looking for a woman with a cattle dog. Keith's sister had written, '*I'll have a cattle dog with me so you can pick me out. Big black and white fella. Can't miss him.*'

And there she was gaily waving a scarf and holding the lead of a rugged kind of dog. She was smaller than Norah had imagined. Her brother had been tall, well-built. This diminutive figure in jodhpurs did not fit Keith's description of a hard-working, hard-riding horse breeder and her short-cropped hair, surprisingly copper coloured, was not at all like Keith's fair thatch. Norah waved back, sought the assistance of a steward to carry her luggage and made for the gangway.

As Marian went with outstretched arms to meet her brother's sweetheart she was remembering what friends had told her about the English. Cold as yesterday's plum duff, they said, sociable as a funnel web spider. She was suddenly attacked by doubt. Would Keith's girl fit into the easy-going ways of Wirrawee? She had a posh look about her.

'Welcome to Australia, Norah.' Her open smiling face and warm hug put Norah instantly at ease. Happily she followed Keith's sister to a siding.

'Sorry about the limo.' Marian released the backboard of a truck and hefted in Norah's suitcases as easily as if they were full of feathers. 'Everyone from Wirrawee who comes to Sydney has a shopping list so it has to be the truck every time.'

Norah was too late with her, 'Let me do that.' The luggage was stowed alongside rolls of wire, cans of kerosene, creosote and sheep dip and the dog last of all.

'I'm tougher than you,' Marian said flatly and held open the passenger door. 'Hop in.' She picked a large bone from the passenger seat and slung it into the back of the truck 'That fella leaves his tucker all over the place. Hope you've brought some jeans with you. That pretty dress is going to take some punishment.'

'I packed my army trousers.'

Marian's eyebrows shot up. 'Something new for the folk at the Creek to talk about. Make yourself comfy,' she added as Norah squeezed herself into the passenger seat. 'We've got a long drive ahead of us.'

Getting comfy was not going to be easy. The iron framework of the seat poked through the plastic upholstery in several places.

'Your legs are too long for that seat,' Marian observed.

Norah was amused by her directness. 'They're regular issue. This seat is meant for half pint people like you.'

In what was already established as a most affable relationship they set off to cross the mountain ridges which separated the coastal plain from its vast hinterland.

In low gear the truck began its long slow climb, leaving the sprawl of Sydney suburbs behind, driving along passes which had been cut through the mountains by early settlers. Convicts had left the marks of their pickaxes as they hacked into age-old rock formations.

The gradient was often alarming. It seemed to Norah that even in low gear the truck would never make it to the top of each rise. Her whitening knuckles as she gripped the edge of her seat were not lost on Marian.

'Don't worry. She always makes it. Too right she's a cow to drive but she hasn't let me down yet. And she's got good brakes. Do you drive, Norah?'

Norah had never even considered such an idea.

'I'll fix that.' Marian turned her curly head and winked. 'That's a promise.'

'Or a threat,' Norah smiled. It seemed the only way to deal with this impish character at whose invitation she had left a dull career in England to totter over the mountains of the new world.

She had Keith's brilliant eyes, sometimes grey as agate, at other times slate blue, but that was the only resemblance Norah could discern. Marian had a heart-shaped face and her nose was small and tip-tilted, not in any way like Keith's long narrow face and hard chin.

'I know what you're up to,' Marian said with engaging candour, 'but I'm not a bit like Keithie.'

21

Norah blushed.

'That's all right. I've been vetting you, too, and I can understand why my brother fell in love with you. Norah, you're a 100 per cent smasher. But, my dear, you won't find anything of Keith in me. We were as different as chalk from cheese. Good mates, though. The best. Bloody war!' she spat out suddenly with surprising venom, at the same time relaxing her firm grip on the steering wheel, and the truck went scuttering in and out of a deep rut. Norah grabbed the dashboard in alarm.

'Sorry, sorry!' Marian was immediately contrite and back in control. 'This is me being selfish. Feeling sorry for myself because the damn Japs robbed me of my super, super brother.' She glanced sideways from under her lids. 'Yet it must be so much worse for you.'

Perhaps she expected a comment but Norah had nothing to say and a little silence fell.

They had reached the top of the ridge and the road ahead flattened out, giving a breathtaking view. 'You wanted to see the bush.' Marian stopped the truck. 'There it is.'

A vast panorama opened up before them of mountain ridges thickly matted with foliage rippling away into the blue distance of the farthest horizons. Not a town in sight, not a building. The undisputed domain of trees since time immemorial. An awe-inspiring sight. Norah was lost for words.

'There are above forty different kinds of eucalypts,' said Marian, 'and turpentines, potosterums and other native trees. Goes up like a bomb in a bushfire. Don't worry,' she threw a quick glance in Norah's direction. 'It's not bushfire season.'

'I'm glad about that.'

'And anyhow the ground has had a good soaking. We've had heavy rains. Washed away a lot of the road. When it rains, it rains rivers but that's better than no rain at all and we do get horrific droughts from time to time. The tanks back home are full now and the creek is running.' She put the truck in gear. 'We're dropping down again now. Heading for that next ridge. We'll take a break there. Stretch your legs. Boil the billy.'

To someone like Norah so lately come from Britain in its battened-down winter the strange natural beauty of the country was intoxicating. Wattles brightened the roadside with their brassy yellow. Their strange musky smell was everywhere. Mop-headed jacarandas punctured the landscape with holes of lavender blue. Flame trees reared scarlet steeples. The thick odour of ferns and the drenching sweetness of ginger plants rose from dank, damp gullies. Citrus plantations on the fertile slopes filled the air with the scent of orange blossom.

'It's all – intoxicating.'

'New smells to you, I suppose.' They were approaching a stand of tall trees at a curve in the road. 'Ever heard a bell bird?' Marian asked. 'They make a tiny chime. Listen hard at the next bend as we drive under the trees. It's a bell bird habitat – right here.'

She slowed down as the road, still descending, led them under a group of tall turpentine trees, their straight trunks opening to a dense and lofty canopy of leaves. She put a finger to her lips.

It was a tiny chime but clear as crystal, a clink which flitted around the treetops with the musical ring of silver spoons.

'Not much to look at,' said Marian. 'We've got more flamboyant birds but none of them can chime like the little bell bird. Hold tight. We're leaving the highway now. It gets pretty rough once we leave the bitumen.' Marian swivelled the truck in and out of a rocky gully and flattened out on to a secondary dirt road. 'There's only one way to take these deep ruts.'

'And that's fast,' Norah finished the sentence for her.

Marian glanced at the outsize watch on her slender wrist. 'We're making good time.' And then, by way of explanation, 'This is Reg's watch. I've bust mine.'

'Who is Reg?'

'My husband. A gorgeous great hunk of a man. Look, I think we'll stop for a break. About another 90 miles to go.' She pulled the truck on to a level space and switched off the engine. 'If you're going to squat somewhere make sure that it's not somebody's home, like a snake's or a nest of ants.'

In the end Norah squatted by the roadside. As if by design, a helicopter appeared overhead.

Marian, blowing a handful of twigs into a flame, doubled up. 'You've been spotted. You'll be on the survey.'

The tea was black and very sweet. Norah peered into the steaming billy. 'There's a leaf in there.'

'Didn't Keith tell you about bush tea? Boil up a gum leaf in the water for a special flavour and also it's supposed to keep the mossies away. They'll go for you, Norah, in a big way. Nothing they like better than new Pommie blood.'

'If they are related to Egyptian mossies,' Norah said, 'they've already sampled mine.'

Marian fished a bag of cakes from a pocket in the truck. 'Did you ever think of writing up your war experiences, Norah? Reckon they'd make interesting reading.'

'Too much tragedy.' Norah shook her head 'Can't face it – but neither can I forget it. Perhaps I will when I am very old. Perhaps the things that hurt now won't matter then.'

Marian looked at her with concern. 'Like Keithie getting killed?'

Norah hesitated. 'That and other things.' Recovering herself she peered into the roadside scrub. 'Are there really snakes about?'

'Heaps of them. But they are more frightened of you than

24

you are of them. You've got to give them the chance to get away. Make a noise and they'll scoot out of your way but if you sit down and pee on them they won't like it and that would be an awkward place to tie a tourniquet.'

Resuming the drive, they left the ridge behind them and dropped down a steep descent to a settlement of single-storey houses built of weatherboard lining the roadside. There were horses and cattle in the fields here and agricultural machinery.

'Paddocks,' said Marian. 'We call them paddocks.'

There was a garage, a general store, a building called the Mechanics' Hall and a very modern motel called the Broken Back Motel which afforded Norah great amusement.

'Who'd want to stay there! The beds must be jolly hard.'

'You goose.' Marian pointed to the ridge they had just crossed. 'That's Broken Back Ridge. It dips in the middle like a woman's back. That's where the hotel gets it name from. Nothing to do with the beds.'

They drove on without another sight of habitation. Norah was kept busy leaping out of the truck to open and shut gates and sometimes to chase sheep off the road. She was hot. Her cotton frock stuck to her back.

'Not long now,' said Marian. 'Back home they'll be listening out for us. You can hear this old banger for miles.'

The afternoon was well advanced when they turned into a private lane, kempt and cared for, bordered with flowering shrubs and leading to a colonial-style homestead built of stone with wide verandahs, standing in the shade of tall spreading trees.

'We're home.' Marian shut off the engine and turned to Norah. 'Here come my folks. My mother and father. The big bloke is my husband. Out you get.'

Norah jumped down from the truck, straightened her skirt and went to meet Keith's family. After a day spent in Marian's informal company all feelings of nervousness had disappeared.

They came towards her, beaming with pleasure, hands extended in welcome. Reg, too, a big hairy man. 'Welcome to Wirrawee.'

But she was not the girl they thought she was.

Three

At that first meeting, Mary and Dan Russell devoured her with their eyes, overwhelmed her with their kindness and warmed her with their hospitality as if she were, indeed, their daughter-in-law of intention.

Tears filled Mary Russell's eyes as she embraced this lovely English girl whom her son had hoped to marry. 'If only Keith were standing at your side now, my dear.'

'It was not to be.' Keith's father, tall and broad as his son had been, gripped her hand and held it long enough to underline the depth of his feeling. His eyes, deep-set in a face browned and wrinkled by a relentless sun, seemed to Norah, by their penetrating gaze, to seek out her integrity but in his voice, pitched low and calm, there was no uncertainty. 'To have you visit us is a rare compensation. You are welcome.'

She was almost undone by their simplicity yet knew that the true facts of her relationship with their son must be concealed if there was to be harmony during this visit. She had made her decision in the first place knowing full well what she was taking on. She must stick to that.

Mary put away her handkerchief. 'I expect you'd like to freshen up, dear. Come along into the cool. You are not used to this heat.' She put her arm through Norah's and led her towards the house. She was short like her daughter but cosily plump whereas Marian was willow slim. 'Marian will show you your room and then we'll have a cup of tea. Reg

27

will bring your suitcase.' She threw a glance of confirmation over her shoulder at her son-in-law who was already taking charge of the luggage.

A broad smile split apart his black beard as he toted the cabin trunk on to his shoulder. 'This is *some* swag for one little English Miss.'

'Sorry,' Norah apologized. 'I didn't know what to bring so I brought everything.'

'Pants and sweaters,' Marian said crisply, following her into the house. 'That's all you'll need. Mine won't fit you.'

A light breeze moved throughout the large, high-ceilinged rooms, gently stirring lacy curtains at the windows and circulating a hint of hay and lavender and baking. Kept darkly cool by wide verandahs, it offered exquisite relief after the sticky heat of the long drive.

Marian stopped at an open door. 'This is your room, Norah'.

There were flowers on the bedside table, a patchwork quilt on the bed, a sheepskin rug on the polished floor-boards. Through the window Norah could see flocks of sheep grazing in sunburnt pastures and, in the distance, the wooded flanks of encircling hills.

'What a lovely room.'

'It was Keithie's room. Now it is yours.' Impulsively she slipped an arm around Norah's waist, giving her an affection-ate squeeze. 'Gee, it's good to have you here, Norah. We're going to have good times together, you and me.'

Norah nodded, feeling suddenly confident of the rightness of everything. This was how it should be. She had made the right decision in coming here. It was right for her and also right for Keith's family.

'Bathroom is at the end of the passage.' Marian made for the door. 'Don't bother unpacking now. Tea'll be ready in a jiffy. Sing out if you want anything. '

Left to herself, Norah turned to the dressing table to lay out hair brush and comb and was confronted by a head and shoulders photograph of Keith, in uniform, as she had last seen him in Cairo. The shock sent the blood rushing to her face. It was as if those steady blue-grey eyes were seeing right through her. The quizzical smile seemed to suggest that he knew what she was up to, how she happened to be there, in his home, in his room, in his country.

Memories of wartime Cairo came to mind; dining with Keith in candle-lit restaurants, dancing on a tiny dance floor crowded with couples in uniform. Champagne corks popping. Egyptian musicians playing mellifluous melodies to relax battle-weary servicemen and lift their hearts. 'The Way You Look Tonight', 'J'Attendrai' and 'We'll Meet Again'. But many of those light-hearted men did not live to see the outcome of the battle of El Alamein.

Were their own letters returned unopened to relatives as hers had been? Stamped 'DECEASED'? There was no arguing with a word like that. It was finite.

When she looked again at the photograph it seemed to her that the eyes were more understanding but sadder. 'Sorry, Keith,' she murmured, sorry for not being able to return his love, even though she was aware that she could not have acted otherwise. She knew now, with absolute certainty, that the physical love between a man and a woman was not for her.

Marian was hollering down the passage, 'Tea up, Norah! On the front verandah.'

As she left the room she closed the door quietly behind her, as though Keith were sleeping there.

The front verandah was a repository for boots, water-proofs, fishing tackle, first aid equipment, piles of maga-zines, tottering stacks of books, a fire extinguisher and odd objects which had no recognized home of their own.

A sagging couch and an assortment of cane chairs invited rest and refuge from the heat of the day in the shade of the overhanging roof. At a table set for tea, Mary was wielding a large tea pot.

'Come along, dear. You must be longing for a cup of tea.'

'Sit by me, my dear,' Dan Russell settled her near his chair. 'Tell us how things are back home? Can they rebuild London after the bombing? Will it ever be the same again? And Coventry, Southampton, all those historic buildings. The pictures in our newspapers horrified us.'

'Australia is lucky to have been spared all that.' Mary was handing cups of tea to Marian to pass around.

'Nothing to do with luck, Mother.' Marian said. 'It was brave guys like Keith who stopped the Japs when they were only a kick away, at Port Moresby.'

'I wouldn't argue with that, Marian,' her mother nodded in agreement, 'so let's be thankful and give Norah a real nice break from all the misery caused by the war.'

Norah rose readily to that. 'The drive here was across some of the most wonderful scenery I could ever have imagined. Australia is so exciting, so very different in every way from England. I am very grateful to you for inviting me here.'

'It's a bonza country,' Dan Russell agreed. 'And a good life if you're prepared to work.'

'Keith often talked about Australia, and especially about Wirrawee and his family, about the things he was fighting for.'

'Where did you meet Keith?' Marian asked.

Norah was prepared for questions like this. 'Our hospital was sent to help the Greeks when the Italians invaded. We were doing a good job until the Germans joined the fight then we had to get out quickly. An Australian officer, despite being wounded himself, helped my friend and me to escape to Crete. That was Keith.'

'He wrote to us about Crete,' said Keith's father. 'German parachutists dropping in hundreds from the skies. He reckoned he was lucky to get out of that alive.'

'Later, Keith turned up in Egypt and we had some happy times together until his regiment was recalled to defend New Guinea. '

They needed to know no more than that but during the silence that followed Norah wondered if she had said too much . . . or too little.

'I did not see him again.'

Dan reached over and took her hand. 'Thank you for coming to visit us. You have helped us all to accept what cannot be altered.' Dan was sixty-two years old, balding, and all the hair he possessed was grey. 'Just to have you here with us is such a comfort.'

A voice inside her screamed a confession, 'I turned him down, your lovely son!' but she kept a closed-in face. 'For me, too, it is a chance to come to terms with my life.'

'Let me fill up your cup, dear,' Mary said softly.

Marian got to her feet and picked up her cap. She had changed into more workmanlike jeans. 'Gotta go and help Reg with the pigs. I'll leave you with Mum, Norah. Back for supper. You relax. Take a shower if you want to. The water tanks are full. There's a *Sydney Morning Herald* kicking about somewhere. Only one day old. See you later.'

'She's got a good man.' Dan drained his cup. 'Strong as an ox. Does the work of two men. He joined us on the station when he and Marian got married and that suited Keith who was bustin' to enlist. There was a little bunch of young blokes round here went off together, just rarin' to get a crack at Hitler. Oh well,' heaving himself out of his canvas chair, 'I reckon I'd have done the same at his age.' He took up his big-brimmed akubra hat. 'I'll leave you ladies to chat. I've got a sick cow. Don't know if she's going to make it.'

'Can I be of some use while I'm here?' Norah offered. 'I'd like to help – if I wouldn't be in the way.'

Dan was looking at her thoughtfully. 'Can you give injections?'

Mary looked shocked. 'Dan! Norah is a nurse, not a vet.'

Norah laughed. 'I have never tried injecting animals but I don't see why not.'

Dan smote his fists together in delight. 'You're on. But I'll let you settle in first. Give you a day or two to get your bearings.'

Left to themselves Mary and Norah cleared away the tea things. 'I was thinking,' said Mary, 'that you might like to look at our family photograph albums? There are some lovely photos of Keith. Have you got a photo of him?'

Norah had to admit that she had not.

'I didn't think you would have. I don't suppose there would be many opportunities during the war, so you must choose one that you would like.'

Page after page of them. Keith on his first pony. Keith carrying his baby sister. Keith riding in the picnic races. Keith coming first in the picnic races, Keith and Marian diving into the river. And then the one she knew, Keith the soldier, going off to fight the war, about to board the *Queen Mary* in Sydney harbour with the chanting, cheering 6th Australian Division. 'Waltzing Matilda' guys from the outback, smarties from Sydney's teeming city squares, men from the Blue Mountains and Botany Bay, from Dog Creek – and Dan Russell's son from Wirrawee Station, all eager to do their bit for the mother country.

Mary, with the album on her knees, turned the pages slowly. The arthritic fingers would linger over certain photographs. From time to time Norah's own eyes would mist over to see the mother so bereft and she surprised herself with the realization that she was not acting. The role of daughter-in-law was not hard to play in this devoted family.

She had survived the initial trials. The family's instant unquestioning acceptance of herself had dismissed her fears. It was with an easy mind that she lay down to sleep that night.

There was a knock at her bedroom door and Marian's damp, curly head poked round. 'Can I come in?' Wrapped in a towelling robe, sharp white against her sunburnt skin, she glowed with health. 'Just popped in to make sure you're comfy.'

Norah smiled. 'I am lying here thinking of the wonderful welcome I've been given and how am I ever to repay such kindness.'

'Just coming to see us is the best thing we could ever have hoped for.' Marian plumped down on the bed. 'So we're going to see that you enjoy every minute of it. Starting tomorrow. Have you got any riding togs?'

'Army slacks and army boots.'

'Crikey! What kind of nag are you used to?'

Norah laughed. 'The last one was a camel.'

'You're tempting me! It would not be impossible.' Marian picked up Norah's hand as it lay on the quilt and held it in her own, small and workworn. 'You know, when I first saw you at the ship's rail this morning, I thought, oh lord, she looks terribly posh. And I find instead you are terribly nice. Sleep well, Norah dear.'

'And you. Goodnight Marian.'

The household was quiet. Norah could hear Reg in the compound talking to the dogs as he locked them up for the night. Outside her screened window night was falling over the paddocks. Twittering birds fussed as they settled in the pepper trees. The piercing bark of a dingo and the deep hoot of a strange bird performed the overture on her first night in Australia. Through her undrawn curtains the unfamiliar sky glimmered with starlight. The constellation she could see was Orion's belt, upside down and renamed the Pan Handle.

She had few thoughts of home. Tomorrow she would ride in the hills with Marian. There was pleasure in that thought. In a funny way, Marian reminded her a little of Cathy.

Four

The household at Wirrawee began the day early, each member about his own business until Lily, Mary's aboriginal helper, would ring the big brass bell on the front verandah for breakfast.

On this fresh autumn morning, while Marian was seeing to the horses, Norah took herself off for a walk in the home paddocks until summoned for breakfast. She was beginning to find her way around the property, which was vast compared with any farm she had known in England.

The sky this morning was azure blue and cloudless. A light breeze, still carrying a coolness from the night, stirred the air with scents of shrubs and flowering trees that Norah had yet to identify. Earthy animal smells drew her to where sheep were resting under a gum tree amongst the detritus of bark, leaves and fallen branches. At her approach they scrambled to their little bony knees and fled, testily bleating at the disturbance. In the topmost canopy of the tree a cacophony of kookaburras cranked up the day's beginning.

It was a morning for looking up as far as the treetops and around as far as the hills, a morning for smelling and feeling how this vast land breathed. The sky was huge. The watching hills stood back from the Wirrawee estate like vigilant giants.

Strangely at ease in surroundings so unfamiliar, Norah walked loosely and with grace. Her lightness surprised her.

Time, she acknowledged, moved slowly here. Those lonely years since the end of the war seemed to matter little now. This, she told herself, is what it means to be carefree and, since it could not last forever, she meant to enjoy to the full every new sensation during her stay. When the time came for her to return to England she meant to take with her such a library of memories as would sustain her in an uncertain future.

If only Cathy were with her, her happiness would be complete. All the same, Marian, with her ready laugh and lively wit, was a delightful companion.

A more serious voice reminded her that, indirectly, she owed her present pleasure to the man whose love she had rejected. This had been his home. She pictured him walking this way, over this tough, springy grass, past tall graceful eucalypts on the way to the dam which he had built with his father.

Keith would have known the name of those birds hanging on the power lines like black rags and of the wild flower that laid a wash of purple over the hill slopes. He must have seen the sun break out, as it was appearing now, from behind the blue line of hills, to illuminate the morning sky. Yet, had he lived, and just suppose she had married him, she would not have made a loving wife. She would not have made him happy. It was not in her make-up. Her disastrous marriage had proved that. Her appreciation of his home, however, would have pleased him. That, at least, was genuine. He had wanted her to see it.

Lost in these thoughts, she almost trod on a patch of mushrooms, fresh as the morning, their clothy white domes sparkling with dew, ready for picking. Marian was on the point of leaving the stable yard and smiled to see Norah make a sling of her skirt and fill it with mushrooms. 'For our breakfast?'

'Yes, and I'm going to cook it. With your dad's home-cured bacon and your mother's sausages it'll be a breakfast fit for a king.'

Marian took her arm. She was thinking, as they walked back to the homestead, 'She is just like a real sister to me. I wish Keith could have seen how happily she fits in.'

Over breakfast at the scrubbed kitchen table where the day's work was discussed it was decided that Marian should take Norah on a tour of Dog Creek. 'You've been here a week,' said Dan, 'and haven't yet met the locals.'

Reg beamed at her over his heaped plate, 'They have a treat in store.'

'A treat for me, too.'

Marian and Reg made an odd pair, or so it seemed to Norah; Marian, so neatly proportioned, always smartly turned out in well-cut jodhpurs and hand-made boots, her movements quick and precise as a ballet dancer, alert as a rabbit, while Reg was like a large and hairy bear let loose in an old-clothes shop. But assuredly he was a friendly and gentle bear and, just as assuredly, he worshipped his little wife. His big, red, crumpled face, of the type which would never adjust to the sun if he were to live to be a hundred, was set by his nature in kindly mode. It was not surprising that such an amiable relationship existed between himself and his in-laws.

There were about five hundred inhabitants of Dog Creek at that time, established graziers like the Russells and a few battlers rearing goats on the poor scrub. Itinerant stockmen, drovers and shearers passed through from time to time, staying a night or two or a week or two, depending on their hire and the season. There was a general store, a garage and one hotel which had seen better days, much better days.

Marian parked the truck in the shade and led Norah in the direction of the river.

Brenda McBryde

'How did it get the name of Dog Creek?' Norah wanted to know.

'Likely some old digger's dog drowned here. Who knows?' Marian shrugged. 'There's a lot of water running in the "wet". Enough to drown a digger *and* his dog.'

On that day what Norah saw was a slackly moving, shallow river with yellow mud flats at its edges. The land around was pitted with excavations.

'It was a beauty spot in my grandfather's time,' said Marian, 'before the prospectors came. Now look at it. They churned it up then cleared off with their gold leaving the creek looking like a disaster area. It's an aboriginal camp now. They seem to like it here, diggings and all.'

She nodded towards a cluster of bark shelters where brown children played and women cooked at open fires. A group of men broke off their conversation to peer at Marian and her companion. Courteously they returned her greeting.

'They will all know who you are by now, Norah.' Marian smiled. 'The bush telegraph will have spread the message that Mr Keith's sweetheart is here from England.'

Norah, caught off guard, flushed crimson and Marian, believing her remark to have been tactless, was instantly contrite. 'Darling Norah, I am sorry. I am so clumsy with words.'

'No, no, Marian,' hastily Norah recovered herself. 'It is all right – really.'

'Yes. You are much braver than I am,' Marian glumly acknowledged. 'I still cry my eyes out when I'm alone, missing him so much. It helps to have you here, bearing up so well.' She took Norah's arm. 'Come on. I'll show you what's left of the town after the gold ran out.'

A cluster of wooden houses, single-storey, tin-roofed, were scattered at random at each side of the so-called 'highway', a wide stretch of graded earth stabilized with a median strip of bitumen.

38

'In the wet,' said Marian, 'when two vehicles meet there's nearly a shootout to see who claims the bitumen. The rest is a quagmire. The road runs from Ironstone, back there,' she thumbed the ridge of hills behind them. 'If we carry on in this direction for another eighty miles we reach Shingles Post and, if you want to know how that got its name, I'd say the postman got the shingles.'

Norah laughed. 'And I'm a raw prawn.'

'I bet you've got places in England with queer names.'

'A little mining village near where I was born is called "Pity Me". Beat that.'

'That's pathetic! You'd never get an Australian place owning up to anything so gutless. More like, "Mud in your eye" or "Get lost!"'

'Maybe one day you will come and stay with me, Marian? I'll show you Little Piddle and Nether Wallop and St Andrew Without, St Andrew in the Wardrobe and Long Bottom.'

'Reckon you come from a land of nutters.' They were reaching the outskirts of the village where the houses were built more closely, each with its small plot of land, enough for a few orange or lemon trees, a vegetable patch or a row or two of vines.

'The houses are built on wooden piles,' Marian explained, 'because of floods and snakes. Both common.'

'You'd better tell me about snakes,' said Norah. 'What do I do if I get bitten?'

'Like I told you, they'll leave you alone if you don't disturb them.'

'But just supposing I – or you – get bitten. Does one still slash open the site with a penknife and suck out the poison or did the Girl Guides get that wrong?'

'Oh, my God, you Poms are so desperately earnest! Your patient would either die of infection from the penknife or bleed to death and you yourself would have a noble funeral.

What you do is stay calm and cross your fingers. It helps if you can identify the snake.'

'The only snake I have ever seen is the picture on a Snakes and Ladders board.'

They had come to a dusty square. 'This place,' said Marian 'is called the Flat, and it is. It is also the business centre of Dog Creek you might say.'

A petrol bowser outside a tin shed identified 'The Loch Lomond Garage. Props P. McKenzie & W. Fraser'.

'Pete and Bluey,' said Marian. 'Cracking good mechanics. They can mend anything on four wheels.'

'Obviously homesick for Scotland.'

'They're third-generation Australians, m'dearioh! Never been to Scotland in their lives.'

'Why the name "Bluey"?'

'Because he's got red hair.'

'Of course.'

Norah's presence was causing something of a stir in the village. Women at windows, in the vegetable patch, women with babies, gossiping, all had a greeting for Marian and an inquisitive eye for her companion. The word spread quickly, the English lass that was Keith Russell's intended before he got killed, was staying at Wirrawee.

'Now, come and admire our shopping centre.' Marian led Norah to a dusty shop window full of faded advertisements and dead flies. 'You can buy anything here. Camphorated oil and liquorice straps, black suspenders and woolly bloomers. The Wilcox family runs it from Grandad down to the last grubby urchin.' Marian pointed to one of them playing with a scabby dog. 'Like that one. Molly, the kids' mother, is supposed to be overseeing their education as laid down by the Correspondence School syllabus but she isn't all that clever herself and she holds the view that the kids learn more by helping in the store, adding up and catching cheats than from any school books. Could be right.'

The Diggers' Hotel, the only public house for miles around, stood a little apart in its own dusty yard where the sole point of interest was the carcase of an ancient vehicle. Old folk who remembered the hotel in its heyday spoke of nuggets of gold changing hands at the poker table, of a place where guns settled arguments. It had been burned down twice and at each rebuilding had lost a little of its former glory as a gold-mining saloon. One-armed Timothy O'Reilly and his apparently motherless daughter ran it.

'He say croc got his arm but Timothy O'Reilly he big liar.'

Norah was suddenly aware of a lanky aboriginal youth at her side.

'He never see no croc. He pitchforked for stealing abo man's gin.'

Marian intervened. 'Miss Norah is from England, Top Hat, and doesn't want to know about that.'

'Why she wear soldier's pants?'

Norah laughed. She had consigned her English cotton dresses to the wardrobe and was wearing her khaki service trousers.

'Miss Norah was a nurse-soldier in the war,' Marian explained. 'The pants are part of her uniform.'

'She come to work in clinic?'

Marian shook her head. 'Miss Norah on walkabout. No working.'

He laughed heartily, showing a mouthful of gleaming white teeth. 'Top Hat on walkabout too. No working.'

'No work. No wages.'

'When hungry I work. Not right now. No hungry.'

Marian pointed to a weatherboard house much in need of repair and paint. 'This is the clinic he's talking about. The doctor visits once a week. Graham Jebb's his name. He lives in Ironstone. We haven't had a resident nurse for some time. That's what Top Hat is on about. The last one died of an excess of rum in her guts.'

'What happens if someone needs a doctor between doctor's visits?'

'Ma or me can hold the fort in the meantime with sticking plaster and a prayer. And there's always the Flying Doctor in an emergency.'

'Abo people got good doctor,' said the young man. 'More better than Dr Jebb. You, soldier-nurse,' he turned to Norah, 'why you not go work in clinic?'

'Oh buzz off,' Marian interrupted irritably, 'and mind your own business.'

Reluctantly, he turned away but not before pointing out the chapel, a rusting shed of corrugated iron supporting a weathervane and a cross. 'That's the Jesus box,' he grinned, his black eyes sparkling with mischief. 'More better sing hymns in the bush. Hot as hell in there.'

'Quite harmless,' Marian assured Norah. 'A marvellous worker when he feels like it. Otherwise a blooming nuisance.'

'What did you call him?'

'Top Hat. That's his name. He's very proud of it. Good job you didn't laugh. Anyhow, he probably thinks you've got a funny name. "Little Miss Moffat",' she joked.

'But that's not my name any longer,' Norah reminded her. 'I've been married, don't forget, briefly.'

Marian caught her breath. 'Sorry. I keep forgetting.'

'I prefer to forget about it.' As always the vision of that awful hotel bedroom rose up, with its plastic flowers and sniggering chamber maid.

Marian took Norah's arm. 'Come on. Back home for Morning Tea. Lily makes melt-in-the-mouth scones.'

Five

Gradually Norah was drawn into all the activities at Wirrawee. Everybody on the station worked hard, played hard and minded his own business. At the end of the day, Dan Russell found relaxation in playing his beloved fiddle. His son-in-law lost more than he won at the card table of the Diggers' Hotel. Mary Russell, the provider of food, first-aid and schooling for aboriginal children, played the piano in the chapel every Sunday and the rosewood harmonium at home.

Norah's help was welcomed in treating wounds and sores of the stock. Caring for animals in place of humans was a challenge she enjoyed. In addition, she dug vegetables and picked fruit for the dinner table; helped Mary to bottle pears and kumquats and make tomato sauce.

'You don't have to work, you know,' said Marian.

'I want to.'

On a quiet mare she accompanied Marian to the back blocks to check fences and take the cattle counts. Cantering through the bush, splashing through creeks, boiling the billy to make bushman's tea, she discovered the wide-open lifestyle of Australia and was utterly seduced by the undemanding solitude of the outback. The unfamiliar birds, so spendthrift with their golden notes; the flowering shrubs and wild flowers quietly blooming at the feet of gum trees, all these filled her with delight. One wonderful day slid seamlessly into the next. She was tanned and

Brenda McBryde

healthy. She could spend all day in the saddle now without aching muscles. Cathy's letters were as eagerly awaited as always but no longer filled her with nostalgia. England was somewhere else. Australia was the here and now and she pushed to the back of her mind the awareness that time was passing and that she must soon make arrangements to go home.

'Where did you learn to ride, Norah?'

'With Cathy. In the desert. There were some really nice mounts for hire in Cairo.'

'As well as camels?'

'I never want to see another camel. Bad tempered beasts. Cathy was thrown by one.' Norah laughed. 'She used up every swear word in her vocabulary. Impressed the young Egyptian attendant no end.'

'You are good friends, you and Cathy, aren't you?'

'We were best friends. Since schooldays. But she's married now.'

The coolness which crept into her voice was not lost on Marian.

They were unsaddling the horses and setting them free to roll in the paddock. 'I'd love to hear about your friends in England sometime, Norah.'

Norah nodded. 'Before I go home, I'll tell you about Cathy and Andrew, and Simon and the others. We had a great time growing up together before the war but they don't belong to Australia. I'll tell you about them some day.'

'You say "Before you go home",' Marian repeated wistfully. 'Do you *have* to go home? Why not stay?'

Norah laughed. 'You're a sweet silly, Marian. I must go home soon. I have already imposed on your parents' hospitality too long.' She laid an arm affectionately about Marian's shoulders. 'But I don't want to lose you.'

'Then stay.'

*   *   *

44

'She's applied to the shipping company for a sailing date, Ma.'

'Well, Marian, it is up to her. After all, she has family back home.'

Marian was cleaning pieces of harness on newspaper spread at one end of the kitchen table while Mary and Lily prepared the midday meal.

'I reckon she doesn't want to go. Reckon she was awful lonely before she came to visit us. Most of her mates had scattered during the war and her best friend, they'd been inseparable since childhood, got married. That is what finally persuaded her to take herself off. She says herself that she was "surplus to requirements".'

'Girl friends have to take a back seat when a husband moves in,' agreed Mary, 'but they don't need to emigrate!'

Marian sighed, 'If only—'

'I know. If only—' Mary swiped the meat knife along the whetstone. 'Flour, Lily. Wholemeal.'

The aboriginal girl moved silently to do Mary's bidding, her lustrous dark eyes and attentive ears missed nothing of the family's affairs. It was like listening to white people's song lines. Strange. Incomprehensible.

Marian went on buffing the pliant leather of her saddle, bringing it to a soft gleam, her mind still on Norah's plans to return to England. 'She's really happy here. Remember what a great time she had at the picnic races? All those lovely bachelor boys from back o' Bourke in their akubras and high-heeled boots, clustering round her like bees at a honey pot. She'd be snatched up if she stayed. I told her she shouldn't spend the rest of her life mourning Keith. She's not cut out to be a spinster.'

'Dad and I will be sorry to see her go,' said Mary. 'She can stay with us as long as she likes.'

'That's the trouble. She feels she is sponging on us.'

Mary puffed. 'Never in the world. The dear girl has

paid her way many times over at Wirrawee. She's out there now, helping Reg. Some of the sheep are flyblown and she seems to be as good with animals as she obviously is with sick people. By rights we should put her on our pay roll.'

'She certainly would not accept that.'

'Well then, if she wants to stay and, at the same time, be independent, why does she not look for a job? Shouldn't be too hard to find work. She can keep Keith's room and pay her way if that would make things easier for her. Chop the onions, Lily, and put them in the pot.'

Marian stopped her polishing, 'Mother! You're a genius. You are right. She might be tempted to take a job and I think I know where there is the very thing for her.'

A disappointment awaited Norah's parents in her next letter home. Edith and Joe Moffat had been expecting confirmation of their daughter's sailing date. Instead Norah wrote to say she had decided to postpone her return to the UK. She had been offered the job of running the clinic in Dog Creek.

'*I will have my own little house provided by the state health authority rent free,*' Edith Moffat read aloud. '*Altogether, Mum, I am very happy to stay here awhile. The Russells are so kind. So don't worry about me. You and Dad must save up and come out here for a trip.*'

'I doubt that very much,' said Mrs Moffat with tight lips and a meaning glance at her husband. She read on. 'She says the house provided for her is a bit neglected but she's got one of the native boys to help her clean it up. Calls himself Top Hat!'

Norah's brother, a proper comic, exploded into laughter.

His mother continued, '*Top Hat is going to fix a temporary shower. (A rope and a bucket of water!)*'

The more she read the more upset Mrs Moffat became.

'The "john", that's what they call the lav, is at the bottom of the pumpkin patch –'
Norah's brother guffawed again but Mrs Moffat was seriously affronted. 'Oh dear. Surely she can do better than that!'

With studied deliberation she folded the letter and replaced it in the envelope. 'Well,' she said, looking askance at her husband, 'what do you make of that?'

Retired chief engineer Joe Moffat took the pipe from his mouth. 'One thing is for sure. She's a good deal happier now in Australia than in postwar Britain.'

Mrs Moffat conceded that. 'But she's a long way from Cathy and the rest of her friends.'

'Things have changed for all of them.'

Edith Moffat sighed. 'I always thought she'd make a good marriage, not that pig-in-a-poke affair with a jumped-up sailor! And now, with the divorce behind her, I hoped she might find a nice, ordinary young man, nothing special, no gold braid or brass buttons. Someone like Andrew Mount, for instance, would have made a good husband for our Norah.'

'He's changed too, has that lad. He's not the cheery bloke who used to take her dancing. His father says five years in a German POW camp have left their mark. He's never married. Jilted by that Jewish nurse, friend of our Norah's.Well, she never married either. She's running that Home for Displaced Persons in Jesworth.'

'Still, Andrew went to see her off when she sailed from Liverpool, don't forget.'

'He'd be handy. He's a GP in that area.'

Edith Moffat reached for her knitting. Nobody needed khaki socks any more but old habits died hard. 'We all thought we'd be in paradise when the war ended but it's left a tail-back of misery for many folks. Here in Eastport there are widows grieving for their men and parents who have lost

their sons and nice young men like Andrew Mount who'll
never be the same again. You were lucky, Joe, to come out
alive and in one piece.'
'Luckier than a lot of my mates.'

It was midsummer in England and the schoolchildren were
on holiday. Their voices came floating over the hedge from
the nearby playground into the garden where Cathy and her
husband were enjoying the sunshine; he stretched out on
a sun lounger, Cathy sitting plumply with her knitting in
a chair that was comfortable both for her and for the
infant she carried. The scents and sights of summer all
around them exquisitely cradled their content. Roses and
Canterbury bells, sweet Williams and hollyhocks massed
together, repaying the tender loving care lavished upon them
with drifts of butterflies, companies of dreaming ladybirds
and the occasional aria from a satisfied bumble bee.

Cathy was re-reading the letter from Norah which had
arrived that morning and had not yet been thoroughly
digested. There was startling news.

'She's staying out there, Ray. She's not coming home.'
Cathy earnestly addressed the newspaper covering her husband's face. 'She's got herself a job, running a clinic. Ray,
she'll miss the christening!'

Raymond Webster lifted a corner of *The Times* to study
his wife's face and judge how stood the wind. Tears,
in her present condition, should be avoided at all costs.
'We could postpone it. How long does she plan to stay
out there?'

'About two years. The Bump would not like to wait that
long to be christened,' she said sadly.

'Did you ask her to be godmother?'
'Of course.'

'Well we can't expect her to come back solely for the
christening but she can still be godmother. Me and the

Bump think that, as she is your oldest friend, she should be godmother. '

'I agree.'

'And, since we're on the subject, what about asking Andrew to be godfather?'

'Good idea. Cheer him up. And it would be a kind of relationship with Norah as godmother. He used to take her out a lot in the old days.'

'Don't make too much of that.' Since he was not a party to 'the old days' she referred to, Ray retired to his cover beneath the newspaper. He was still a little cautious about direct sunlight.

'OK, you ask him then.' Cathy went back to the letter. Norah's job sounded really interesting.

> There's everything from snake bite to prickly heat. People get trampled by steers and kicked by horses, bitten by spiders and have their ears torn off in a friendly fight. I never know what is going to turn up and I love it. I'll give it a go, perhaps for a couple of years.

Cathy could understand why Norah was anxious to move out of the Russell homestead. Living with the family of the man whose love she had spurned must surely have been embarrassingly awkward at times. Norah confirmed this.

> Marian keeps his favourite saddle polished, on its own special hook in the stables, always with a fresh posy of flowers. They are wonderfully kind to me but I just had to get away from that accusing stare from every photograph of Keith. I will be better on my own in my 'humpy' as Mary calls it and I am doing a worthwhile job.

49

Norah had been the envy of the Sisters' Mess in Cairo when the handsome Australian asked her to marry him and she amazed her friends when she turned him down. Cathy also witnessed Norah's misery when he was killed. She may not have wanted to marry him – to marry anyone – Cathy now thought, but Norah had welcomed his friendship.

'Australia has been good for Norah,' she addressed the newspaper. 'She sounds really happy.'

'Well, that's an achievement.'

'What d'you mean?'

'Well, my touchy darling, you have to admit she was a sad sack before she left.'

'It was that awful man she married.' Norah's wedding came to mind. The groom in his fine feathers. '"Cock o' the Midden" my dad called him. And Norah's parents, looked if they were attending a funeral not their daughter's wedding.' Norah herself, she recalled, had been pale as a lily and trembling like an aspen tree.

Cathy pulled herself back to the present. Rhythmically the page of newspaper fluttered and settled on her husband's face. The thoughts she was about to convey died on her lips. Sternly she accused him. 'I believe you've been dozing there while I have been working my fingers to the bone to clothe your child.'

He jerked alert. 'It's going to be too hot for all those knitted boots and things.'

'It's a November baby! How would you like to go about with nothing on but a nappy – in November?'

'I wouldn't want to be seen in knitted boots either.'

Cathy sighed. 'I can see you are going to be one of those really irresponsible fathers.'

'But indispensable for the purpose of procreation.'

Six

D r Jebb, who had done his MB in Sydney and his FRCS in London, reckoned he knew a fair bit about the inhabitants of both places. He had been mighty pleased when Marian Reed told him about this English nurse who was interested in running the Dog Creek clinic. He was delighted. Having a qualified nurse there would halve his work, but when he met her his hopes were dashed. He gave her a month, maybe not as long as that, before she would hand in her chips. A blonde and beautiful Pom in her crisp white uniform and blancoed shoes on a first visit to Australia, taking on the raw material of Dog Creek? Not likely. The roughnecks coming in with broken noses and slashed faces would make mincemeat of her. They were used to being shouted at, like the last old biddy, before they heard a single word. That old girl could handle anything till she got the shakes and retired to a home for inebriates. This lass, with her posh voice and Pommie ways, would never keep them in order.

But she did. The rough and ready station hands, jackeroos and aboriginal stockmen did as they were told – and quick. The doctor's estimated toleration time went by. She stayed and became part of the scene.

Funny a sheila like her couldn't get herself a man. Graham Jebb maintained a lively interest in women in general and pretty ones in particular. OK, he was at the wrong end of the fifties but that didn't mean he was going to sign up for celibacy. Not by a long chalk.

He was more than a little intrigued with his new nurse. She'd been engaged to Keith Russell from Wirrawee. Everybody knew that. There was a rumour, however, that, when he was killed, she jumped into marriage with some guy she'd known during the war and out again quick as a cat from a bucket of hot water. Funny that. He might have had a go himself, but he had a wife of his own somewhere and he believed in letting sleeping dogs lie, or, to put it more accurately, sleeping bitches. Anyway, the new nurse was a mite standoffish with him. Didn't seem to be bowled over by his irresistible charm. Could be she was not in a hurry to get caught again.

As for the residents of Dog Creek, they had a lot of time for the English nurse at the clinic. Keith Russell was the Creek's own war hero and, if Sister Norah was good enough for him, they reckoned she'd do for the Creek.

The clinic which was now Norah's concern consisted of an office doubling as consulting room, a treatment room and a small waiting room equipped with sad old chairs whose stuffing provided a home for mice. The dwelling allocated by the shire council for the resident nurse was a weatherboard extension to the clinic. It had been unoccupied for the last ten years and needed a heap of attention.

Norah was delighted with it. Mary Russell was horrified. She looked at the kitchen with its torn linoleum floor covering and ancient cast-iron stove, at the bathtub, full of spiders and empty gin bottles, in an alcove behind a ragged curtain. 'One tap,' Mary pointed out, 'and that's cold.'

Norah was in what was to be her bedroom, a poky little place with walls of a bilious green which she was covering with a coat of white paint.

'Norah, my dear, you can't live in this humpy! You know you can have Keith's room at Wirrawee for as long as you like.'

Norah's reply had to be courteous but none-the-less firm or her move to independence would come to nothing. 'Now that I've got this job,' she explained, 'it's better that I live near the clinic.'

A fancied rebuff registered in the eyes of the older woman. Norah laid a hand on an arm that was wrinkled and browned by almost sixty Australian summers. 'I can never repay you for your kindness, Mary, but I have to stand on my own feet. I'll be at hand to help at Wirrawee whenever you need me.'

'And even when we don't,' put in Marian. 'You're on a short lead.'

Now that she was about to leave Wirrawee Norah was struck with a sudden doubt. 'We'll still ride together, Marian? After I've moved?'

And Marian had been reassuringly positive. 'Sure thing. You haven't roped your first brumbie yet. That I have to see. You're not going to get rid of me. I'll be around, getting in your hair. I'll help in the clinic if you're really pushed. But the doc always yells at me because I can't roll up a bandage without dropping it. That is your job now and he won't dare to tell you off, that's for sure.'

'He won't need to. I can roll up a bandage.'

Seeing that Norah had made up her mind to live there, the whole Russell family set about transforming the grubby little shack, Mary hanging curtains which she had run up on her sewing machine, Marian fixing a mosquito net where the bed would go, Dan clearing a path through the scrub to the 'john' ('Got to get your priorities right'). Top Hat made an important contribution by clearing a colony of possums from under her roof.

'Possum pee on your ceiling,' he pointed out when she demurred at the thought of ousting these dear little furry-tailed creatures from their home.

Reg was working on the stove, clearing the flue of birds' nests and rubbish. 'You've got a cracker oven, Norah,' he reassured her once he'd got a good fire going, 'and a boiler. I'll run a pipe to your tub.'

Norah knew they were doing it for Keith. Her debt to his family grew daily. A bed and a chest of drawers arrived from Wirrawee. 'Surplus,' said Mary. 'Funny old stuff that came over from Ireland with my great grandfather in the potato famine. Perhaps you can find a use for it.'

Nevertheless it was Top Hat's gift that took first prize for originality.

The kookaburras had scarcely begun their morning racket and the dew still sparkled on the Christmas bush in the stock-yard at Wirrawee when, one morning in late September, Reg got the truck ready for a trip to Parramatta, near Sydney, where an auction sale of railway fittings was advertised. Useful items for the estate like rope, buckets, paint and bits of equipment could often be bought at a knock-down price at such sales. He zipped up his jacket, for the morning was fresh, and started the engine as quietly as possible as the family was still abed. No one was stirring as he drove through the village but a figure was waiting at the side of the road near the river crossing signalling for a lift.

'You want a lift somewhere, Top Hat?'

Without hesitation, Top Hat opened the cab door and climbed into the passenger seat. 'Parramatta sale, along o' you, mister.'

A cocked eyebrow was Reg's only response as he got on the way again.

'You an' Mister Dan been talkin' 'bout it,' Top Hat explained. 'And I think Top Hat go too.'

'You got your eye on something special, boy?'

Top Hat was not to be drawn. 'If somethin' good comes, I buy. '

Reg smiled. 'You won the lottery!'

On their return late that evening, Top Hat leapt from the truck and made straight for Norah's humpy to present his acquisition. 'Ladies have proper seats on the john,' he informed her with a nice show of delicacy as he handed her a handsome lavatory seat made of cedarwood and fitted with brass hinges.

Norah treated the matter very seriously. 'Thank you very much, Top Hat. This is a beautiful piece of furniture. I will ask Mr Reg to fix it for me.'

'You should have seen him go, Norah,' Reg was convulsed after Top Hat swaggered off, 'banging away with his bid till the other bidders dropped out. They were all having a good laugh at his expense. "Where you going to put it, son? In the bush?" But Top Hat doesn't say a word, just walks away with what the auctioneer called "this desirable item" tucked under his arm, very dignified. He's got class, that boy.'

With the gradual acquisition of little items of comfort and colour Norah's place was beginning to look less of a 'humpy' and more of a home. An invitation was sent to the residents of Wirrawee to attend her house-warming. There were seats for everyone, given that she and Marian sat on camouflaged oil bins. What started with tea and cakes ran into overtime and finished with gin and beer, cards and music. Dan had been instructed to bring his fiddle. It was altogether a most successful launch of Norah as a householder.

The hour was late when her guests prepared for home. As she was leaving, Mary took her hand and whispered, 'I will always think of you as the daughter-in-law I was meant to have.'

And Norah could respond in all sincerity with a daughter-in-law's embrace. She could not have felt more affection for this family had she been a legitimate daughter-in-law.

From her newly painted doorway she watched Marian and Reg go hand in hand through pools of patchy moonlight to where the Rover stood, its gleaming dark green bonnet spattered with petals from the jacaranda tree.

'No truck tonight?' Norah called out.

'Mother demands the Rover when we go visiting Norah. You're special.'

'You got it real nice, Norah.'

'Thank you, Reg.' Norah laughed out loud to see Reg, with his creased and dimpled face, transformed by the moonlight into a genial gnome. 'You did most of the work. I can never thank you enough.'

After they had driven off and the last well-bred murmur of the Rover's engine died away, Norah continued to stand, looking out over the quiet countryside. The night breeze sighed over the deserted streets of Dog Creek sending a tin can rattling down the bitumen, disturbing a grumpy watchdog. From somewhere in the rustling dark came the weird call of the mopoke, a fellow creature in solitude. Norah was alone but not lonely. Not lonely any more.

'Are you happy out there?' Cathy had asked. How could she be otherwise. She had made many friends in the village. She had found challenging employment. She had a home and she had Marian. Only one thing could have added to her happiness, to have Cathy here with her, together, as they had always been.

She reminded herself that Cathy's baby was due any day now. She would ask Marian to drive her to Ironstone to buy a present and wondered if Andrew would attend the christening. After all, he was the godfather.

She turned her back on the clothy darkness of the night and went indoors. Her little wooden house under its tin roof shrugged and settled in the midnight wind for all the world like a ship at sea. She felt safe here, and loved.

She plumped up the cushions on the sofa as her mother

had done every night of her married life and prepared for bed. She opened the curtains at her bedroom window and let the moon come in and moonbeams, alighting on her nightdress, turned it to silver.

Seven

Three weeks till Christmas and the mercury was rising. Out on the Flat the dazzle of light on rock-hard earth hit the eyes like a physical blow. Bubbling bitumen stuck to the tyres of the postman's bike as he pulled up at Norah's gate. She thrust her spade into the patch of garden she was preparing for vegetables and went to see what he had left for her in the oil drum which served as a mail box.

Letters from home were red-letter days, especially so at Christmas time. This was by no means the first Christmas she had spent away from her family. During the war she was usually serving overseas at this season, but always with Cathy. That was the difference.

There were two letters for her, one from her mother who kept her informed about family affairs and never failed to send her a copy of the *Eastport Gazette*. The other letter, she recognized with a little thrill of pleasure, was addressed in Andrew's medical scribble. His letters were few and far between and she guessed that the christening of Cathy's baby would be the subject of this one. As godparents she and Andrew had a shared interest.

She moved into the perfumed shade of the pittosporum tree to read his letter in comfort. Not even the wide brim of her straw hat could cut out the glare of the sun this morning.

The image of Andrew as she remembered him before the war was in her mind, the glamour boy of the hospital where she and Cathy were training, 'a promising student, a deft surgeon,' the chiefs said, but the wasted years spent in a POW camp and the cold shoulder from the woman he loved had left him disillusioned with life in general, almost a recluse in his country practice in north-west England. Cathy kept in touch with him. He got on well with her husband, as well he might, since Ray had been a patient of his at one time. She slit open Andrew's letter.

> Cathy has produced a fine boy. Mother and baby doing well. Ray is over the moon. You remember, as I do, that very sick soldier in the side ward of Eastport General, wasting away with TB lungs. To see him now, holding his healthy son in his arms, is to witness a miracle. They have called him Philip Raymond. You and I, Norah, had not the advantage of these marvellous life-saving drugs when we were trying to treat tuberculosis.
>
> Cathy missed you. It was a nice party. Eric and Rosemary travelled from Northumberland. Alec sent a wire from Canada. I was glad to get up to date with them. A bright spot in my dreary calendar. Cathy tells me you are running a clinic. Good for you. Sometimes I envy you.

'Hi there!' Marian, calling from the fence as she tied up her horse, broke into her thoughts.

'Superb timing,' Norah stuffed the letters into her pocket. 'I need a tea break. I got up extra early to dig this patch before the heat of the day but I've lost that race. Come on in.'

'We've killed a pig.' Marian lifted a bundle from her saddlebag. 'Put this lot in your freezer.'

They carried the bundle of meat indoors to the freezer which, like so many of Norah's household goods, was a gift from the Russells.

'How on earth did the early settlers manage without refrigeration?'

'Salted and smoked and invented the ice box.'

'I bet there were some nasty intestinal episodes.' Norah shifted the kettle on to the hob.

'Their home-brew would kill any lurking bugs.'

'I got two letters from home today. One from my mother and one from Andrew.'

'Your doctor friend. When are your parents coming out to visit you?'

'Maybe next year. My father retires then. I'm trying to persuade them. My mother's not keen.'

'Bloody hot in this kitchen.' Marian whipped off her canvas hat revealing damp curls plastered to her head. The tin roof above their heads creaked and buckled under the heat. 'Are you regretting your move here, Norah? Not many creature comforts and December's our hottest month.'

'It was pretty hot in the desert. Come on,' Norah picked up the two mugs of tea. 'It's cooler outside.'

Cooler and fresher under the dense dark canopy of the pittosporum tree. From here they could watch the butcher birds disporting themselves in the bird bath Norah had constructed. 'Lucky little birds. It must feel wonderful to cool off the hot feathers under their wings. My own wings are pretty sticky.'

'You need a pool, Norah, and some ceiling fans. You certainly must have a fan in the kitchen. I'll tell Reg.'

'For goodness sake! I don't need pools or fans. Reg has done more than enough for me. I bless him every day for my shower. That is my lifesaver.'

'He's a man of many talents, is my Reg.'

For an instant Norah felt a flicker of envy that this marriage was so demonstrably rock solid. Whenever Marian spoke of her husband a look of tenderness crossed her face. The eyes which could flash ice when she was angry, like when she found a stockman ill-treating a horse, were soft and tender for Reg. And, for him, she was the pivot of his being, his love.

'And you let me take advantage of Reg's kind heart, Marian. I've done nothing to deserve the help he gives me.'

'We all remember Keithie.'

That was it.

Little gaps in the conversation like this left Norah floundering. Some comment was expected of her but her mind would go suddenly into neutral and she would be tongue-tied.

Marian stepped in. 'It must have been difficult to treat casualties under canvas in the heat of the desert.'

'We got used to it, flies, bugs and rats and not much water. I think you can get used to anything. It was much worse for the wounded.'

Marian was silent, thinking of her brother. Who looked after him when he lay dying on the Kokoda trail? What were his last thoughts before leaving us all for ever – of Mum and Dad? Me perhaps? And, certainly, of Norah.

'Have a biscuit,' Norah passed a plate. 'I made them myself. They'll break your teeth.'

'What's the news from England? Did your friend Andrew go to the christening?'

Norah nodded. 'The baby's name is Philip Raymond. Andrew says mother and baby are doing well.'

'Pity you couldn't be there – your best friend's first baby.'

'Oh well. Things don't always work out the way you want them to.'

'Was it the cost of the fare that stopped you? You know I would willingly have helped.'

'No, nothing like that.' Norah shifted uneasily on her perch, an oil drum spread with the *Farmers' Weekly*.

61

'Cathy's marriage was a shock to all her old friends. We expected her to marry Simon Poole, one of us. He had been in love with Cathy for ever. Used to meet her after school. Took her to the pictures on a Saturday night and, even on active service during the war, he managed to keep in touch with her. He would suddenly turn up at our desert hospital whenever he could borrow transport. And then, when the war ended, she married an ex-patient with a history of pulmonary tuberculosis.'

'So he obviously survived the original prognosis.'

'Oh yes. New drugs.'

'Hard luck on the other bloke,' Marian shrugged, 'but that's the name of the game. After all, it was Cathy's choice. I don't see why it should bother you, Norah.'

Norah's brows came down. 'Her husband has come between Cathy and me. It would have been so different had she married Simon. Simon is an old, old friend and I am so sorry for him.'

'And for yourself,' Marian said sharply.

Norah coloured and was silent.

Marian pursued the subject. 'Look at it this way, if you had married Keith, would Cathy have minded?'

Norah hastened to refute such a suggestion. 'She liked him very much. She wanted me to marry him.'

Marian's wide eyes, momentarily questioning, searched Norah's face, then briskly returned to a more uncritical mood. 'Sorry, darling, I didn't mean to pry.' She got to her feet. 'Got to go. I'm taking the truck to Sydney tomorrow. Anything you need? Any medical supplies?'

Norah walked with her to the tethered horse. 'Some onion sets please and four second-hand chairs for the clinic waiting room.'

Marian let out a peal of laughter. 'Crikey! You're a new broom all right.'

'The present seats are a disgrace.'

'Who's going to pay?'

'I will send the bill to the Shire Health Authority.'

'No harm in trying but they are fossilized from the neck up.' She hoisted herself into the saddle and looked down with affection on Norah. 'You know, you have surprised us all, the way you settled so easily in Australia and in this one-horse town particularly. When I first met you at the ship, you seemed sort of – adrift. Were you?'

'Too right, mate.'

Marian laughed. 'We'll make a good Aussie of you yet.'

'Thank your parents for the pig.'

'OK. I'll be off. I'm breaking in Star's foal. She's as cussed as her mother.' She gave her horse a touch of the boot and, as he made to walk off, Marian twisted in the saddle. 'What became of the bloke who didn't win fair lady? Simon, was it?'

'He was devastated, joined the regular army after the war and is serving in Berlin with the army of occupation at present.'

'Did he marry?'

Norah shook her head. 'I don't know. Probably not. Andrew would know. They are good friends, still in touch.'

Eight

The clinic, under Norah's direction, had taken on a more professional air. Carbolic soap and methylated spirit ensured that here was no habitat for germs. Flowering shrubs in her garden provided sprays for the waiting room. Comfortable chairs replaced the broken-down originals and Norah's cat dealt with the mice. Norah herself, in a smart uniform delivered by mail order from David Jones' store in Sydney, neat as a new pin, completed the transformation of the old neglected medical post.

Reports of the smashing nurse at Dog Creek attracted hopeful young farmers from far and wide, frequently with suspiciously vague symptoms. They were dealt with coolly and, if they persisted, she simply made the medicine nastier. All of this provided great entertainment for Marian.

'Seems like there was room for only one man in her life,' said her mother.

There were plenty of genuine illnessess and accidents to keep Norah occupied, some of them way outside her previous experience, as when one of Marian's horses tore its neck badly on a barbed-wire fence. The tear was long and jagged and would never heal without stitching. Norah had stitched soldiers' wounds, little boys' knees and women's post-labour tears but never a frightened stallion with a wild and rolling eye.

In all likelihood, without Marian's support, she would have taken to her heels and run for cover but together they were able to hold him while she administered an anaesthetizing injection. The powerful legs folded beneath him and he lowered his sweating body to the ground with a gentle groan of displeasure. Norah settled herself, cross-legged, on the grass beside him. With his truly noble head, docile now, lying by her knee, she began to stitch the tough hide, pulling together the two edges in a neat seam, all the while keeping an alert eye on the dilations of his deep chest.

She was pleased with the finished appearance. 'My mother would be proud of a seam like that.'

Marian was equally proud of her. 'I bet your Cathy's never stitched up a stallion.'

'Stitching up horses was not in our training syllabus. She could have done it, though,' she added loyally.

Clinic day was organized with military precision. Three years in the army had left their mark on Norah. From the clinic door she could spot the small puff of dust which heralded the doctor's approach as his ancient Holden climbed out of Emma Gully. The puff of dust grew to a cloud as the road flattened and accompanied the doctor all the way to Dog Creek. By the time he reached the clinic the kettle was boiling and Graham Jebb's pot of tea was waiting for him.

He found appointments for his weekly visit neatly entered in a ledger, his patients sitting, good as gold – most of them sober – in the waiting room or in the shade by the door. There was hot water and clean towels, sterile instruments and a decent light to work by. She was efficient – and correct. No bottom-pinching with this young lady. He hadn't even dared to try.

As time went on, Graham Jebb learned to trust her judgement completely, discovering that she was perfectly capable of dealing with most emergencies occurring between his visits. If necessary she would contact the flying doctor service and arrange for her patient to be transferred to hospital. There were occasions, not often, when he'd been a bit heavy on the grog the night before and missed the clinic visit altogether and she just carried on without him. He frankly admitted that she was worth her weight in gold in this dead and alive hole and he prayed she would never go back to England.

A dramatic improvement in Norah's personal accommodation came about as a gift from a grateful patient, who was also the local rogue.

Daddy Watts rode into Dog Creek soon after midnight from the boundary rider's hut where he lived. Norah woke to see his big red face poking through her bedroom window, a remarkable apparition considering that the window was several feet above ground.

'Get yersell outa bed!' he was hollering. 'I gotta have some physic. I'm crook in the guts.'

Gripping his stomach and rolling from side to side in the saddle of a magnificent horse, probably stolen, he was setting up such a row that Norah wasted no time in grabbing an overall and opening up the clinic. The smell of him was stupefying, reminding her of the coalhouse back home after a fox had spent the night there.

'What have you been eating?' she demanded once she had hiked him on to the couch. Prodding the awesome expanse of rumbling, rattling belly for a sensitive spot was like poking a jelly.

'Summat that black bitch served up. Called it possum pie but I reckon it was a rat. She dint eat none herself. She be tryin' to do me in, and that's a fact.'

The castor oil that she gave him did the trick in spectacular fashion and he was her grateful handyman from that moment on. Services of the nurse were provided free to the people of Dog Creek even when requested in the middle of the night. That part of Norah's duty was covered in her comprehensive salary but Daddy Watts, rogue though he was, was not to be found lacking in appreciation.

'Just you call on me if you want summat done,' he vowed and that was how she got her nice little sitting room with verandah built as an extension to her kitchen. He could do a good job when he felt like it, when he was sober, which was not often, or when not occupied with one of his black gins, and that was not often either. His nickname derived from all the little brown piccaninnies running around Dog Creek who were the fruit of his overactive loins.

He kept his word to Norah, however, and built her a room that she could be proud of. He built it of split pine logs and sealed them with pitch. He built a fireplace with a good brick chimney so that she could light a fire on cold nights. The floor was of cedar planks which he had 'rescued' from a tumbledown colonial house in an abandoned block. Norah polished them to a rich glow and laid down her only extravagance, a creamy Chinese rug which she bought on a trip to Ironstone with Marian. She bought a second-hand settee from Sandy Wilcox at the store and she had a 'room'. Her 'salon', Marian called it. It was her delight, a cosy place where she could sit with her friends over a drink and watch the sun go down over the darkening hills.

She spent her time between the clinic and Wirrawee. She and Marian explored new trails in the bush, riding through carpets of crackling gum leaves, the horses picking their delicate way through bark and fallen branches which it is in the nature of such trees to shed. As they rode side by side they would from time to time disturb a dozing snake. Sometimes a family of grazing kangaroos would be startled into wild, leaping flight.

The bush was full of bird calls, the crack of the whip bird, the cackle of the kookaburras, the beautiful descending cadences of the rainbow bird. Norah spared scarcely a thought for the sparrows and starlings of her native land, for the tidy front gardens edged with London Pride, for neat parks and Victorian bandstands and queues at the bus stop, but she continued to press her parents to visit. Her father had now retired. They should make the trip before they grew too old, she told them.

By this time it would have been hard for a stranger to pick Norah out as an Englishwoman, though her cool English accent would always give her away. She was as tanned as Marian and an excellent rider. She could now drive the truck as well as the tractors and so was able to make a useful contribution to the labour force at Wirrawee, transporting stock to and from the local saleyards, collecting equipment for Reg's pigs from Ironstone agricultural depot, picking up extra feed for the horses. She enjoyed this side of her work as much as her clinic duties.

She and Reg worked well together. His skill in handling sick animals was impressive. With his rough workaday hands he would gentle a cow with milk fever or a new-born lamb as tenderly as its dam. Pity there were no children, she thought. At least, not yet and Marian, at thirty-three, should not put off starting a family indefinitely, if she meant to have one. Reg would make a devoted father.

'Do you belong to these parts, Reg?' she asked one day when they were working together in the long shed, unloading a delivery of cattle cake. She was curious about his background, for he seemed to lack any relatives in the area.

'I'm from Queensland,' he said. 'Came here as a jackeroo. Found a bonza boss in Dan.'

'And married his daughter,' Norah smiled.

He laughed. 'And married his daughter,' then added seriously, 'Changed my life, that did. To think that a lovely girl like her would look twice at a bloke like me was like a wild dream.'

'You shouldn't belittle yourself.'

'It was my family that did the belittling.' He put his shoulder to a heavy sack of feed. 'Now don't you go lifting these, Norah. If you bust your back we'll have to send for Graham Jebb and you wouldn't like that. You stand by with the scoop and fill the bins.'

Norah picked up the scoop and started shovelling the sweet-smelling cubes of cattle cake into the metal bins. 'Your family should come and see how you and Dan run this station. There'd be no belittling by any of them. Have they ever been here?'

'Oh no. In their eyes working on the land is for peasants. My father was a medical specialist. My two sisters, both brainy, are holding down well-paid jobs in the business world. According to them I am a scumbag. No university degree. No crash course on how to make money. A dead loss.'

'Then they are not clever at all, if that is what they think.'

He flashed her a grateful smile. 'So I packed my swag and quit. Left them to commune with their hot-air merchants and their toffee-nosed wives.' He paused for breath, resting his elbow on a bale, and a dreamy look came into his eyes. 'I fell hopelessly in love with Marian the first time I clapped eyes on her. Who wouldn't? Just the most lovely woman I had ever met. But what in the world did she see in me? I've not had much in the way of an education and I'm no Clark Gable to look at.' With a confident grin he challenged Norah, 'But she loves me.'

Norah laughed. His transparent happiness was infectious. 'I know she does. She's got a good man and she knows it.' She bent to her task again. 'Have you taken her to meet your family?'

Reg tossed a huge bale as if it were filled with cotton wool. 'My father never knew nor cared if I had a wife. He's dead now. I did not take Marian to meet my sisters. I was not going to let them patronize her.'

69

'What about your mother? Surely she cares about you?'

'She lives in a retirement home. I go to see her every Christmas. She doesn't remember me.'

If there could have been a light in that dark story it would have been the meeting between his mother and Marian. Too late now.

'So your father never knew that you are now an equal partner with Dan of this 10,000 acre estate? That you are accountant and financial adviser to the property?'

'I like working with figures,' he explained apologetically. 'At school I was good at maths. I just didn't want to work for my living in a stuffy office.'

The understanding between them was satisfactorily uncomplicated.

'Well, it all turned out right in the end, Reg.'

'Norah. I'm a lucky man. I'm singing.'

The firm friendship which had developed between her daughter and Norah was a source of great comfort to Mary. After a ride the two young women would come back to the homestead to prepare the tea and Mary, sitting at her crocheting and listening to their chatter, would imagine another figure there, that of her son, bringing chairs for the girls, beer for his dad. But that sort of thinking got her nowhere, like picturing a bassinet on the verandah and the shawl of finest merino she would crochet. Then she would quietly sigh. There was no sign as yet of her ever becoming a grandmother. She would not pry. There were some questions not even a mother should ask.

She worried, too, about Norah. Several unattached men had shown an interest in her but she gave them no encouragement. She was thirty-six years old and clearly was not seeking a husband. She was still a pretty woman, though the lustre of her hair had been dulled by the sun and her English complexion was parched, but the warmth of her smile made friends wherever she went. All those who needed her care, sick people of Dog Creek and those too old to look after themselves, loved the English nurse. Watching Norah as she taught aboriginal children some of the games that English children play, Mary would shake her head. She should have children of her own.

The loss of her son, Keith, faced Mary every day in so many ways. The pain would never diminish. When she looked at Norah her heart called out, 'What a waste of a lovely daughter-in-law.'

Norah had lived that lie most successfully.

Concern about Marian's childlessness was also exercising Norah's mind. Hesitating to presume upon their friendship, yet knowing that there were many ways of helping infertile women, Norah eventually decided to mention the subject. She chose a time when, pleasantly tired after a long, hot ride, they were leading the horses back to the yard.

Marian responded with characteristic candour. 'That's not the trouble, Norah. There's no shame attached to a woman who is infertile but a man hates to admit he is impotent.'

After that there was nothing more to be said.

'What are you two gossips arranging now?' Reg fell into step between them, placing an arm around each shoulder.

Norah flushed with guilt lest he had overheard their discussion but Marian was not in the least put out. With a huge wink at Norah she declared without the slightest hesitation, 'A date for you to take us both to the Picnic Races at Brough End next Saturday, honey. I'm going to enter Norah in the Barrel Race,' which allowed Norah to close the subject in a loud protest.

On the quiet, Joe Moffatt had been making his own enquiries concerning a possible discount on the fare to Australia before bringing up the subject with Edith. Five years had passed

71

since their daughter left for Australia, and, what with one thing and another, Edith's back for a start, and the fact that neither of them was getting any younger, he was seriously considering a trip to Australia. The shipping line, he discovered, was prepared to offer a handsome concession in view of his wartime experience as chief engineer on a tanker.

'So they should,' said Edith. 'Not to mention your service on cargo ships since the war. I would never have entertained the idea of going to Australia at the full price but this seems a very reasonable offer and I must say I'm worrying myself sick to see our Norah. Not to stay long, just to see that she's all right. Then I won't mind coming away back to England and leaving her there to live her own life the way she chooses.'

Norah was delighted and went straight away to book a room for them at the Diggers' Hotel but Mary would have none of it. 'Allow Norah's mother and father to sleep in that flea pit! Not likely. Dan and I will be glad to have them stay with us at Wirrawee.'

But Norah's father was a man used to making his own decisions and had rather looked forward to sampling the delights of an old gold-mining saloon. In his eyes the lack of paint, the shredding doormat and the broken window mended with brown paper was historic and romantic. Mary overrode such fancy nonsense with her common sense but he was reluctant to give in without at least a show of independence, '"Clean beds," it says on the door, Mrs Russell. "Good tucker."'

To Mrs Moffatt's great relief, Mary firmly demolished these claims. 'Good tucker maybe,' she pronounced. 'That lass of his can no doubt cook a good steak. But clean beds never. I wouldn't put my kelpie bitch in her sheets. You'll come as our guests to Wirrawee and that will be our pleasure.'

They made Edith and Joe as comfortable as they knew how, but there was relief on the visitors' faces when the time came for them to return to Britain. They had enjoyed their time with Norah, meeting her friends, visiting the clinic. Norah and Marian had taken them into the bush, introduced them to Australian birds and animals, to rearing hillsides of volcanic origin and rocks decorated with the paintings of the aboriginals. But the heat and the flies, the possible encounter with a snake or poisonous spider, even the tame goanna who lived on Norah's verandah ('Mother, he's my fly catcher!') made every day a survival test. They were glad to return to England knowing that Norah was happy and among friends.

For Joe Moffatt, a man of the sea, the Australian way of life had been a revelation, typified for him in the character of Dan Russell. There had been an instant understanding between these two men each finding out where the strengths of the other lay and what difficulties had been faced and overcome.

'He built that house, you know, Edith, with his own hands. Every stick and stone of it. Dan and his son raised the stock, dug the dam, built the yards. Australia's like that. You don't send for the builder or the chimney sweep or the fencer. You roll up your sleeves and do it yourself. My,' this with a deep sigh, 'if I were younger . . .'

'What a great loss to them to lose their son,' sighed Edith.

'Could have been our son-in-law and there would have been nothing wrong with that.'

'Funny she never talked about him.'

'That's our Norah.'

'Looks like she's set in her ways now.'

'An old maid, and her such a bonny lass.'

'Aye, well, Joe Moffatt; you'll no doubt call me a fool but I'll have my say and then it will never cross my lips again.'

Her husband looked at her in surprise. His wife was not given to making weighty statements. 'What's biting you? Spit it out.'

'There was something happened to our Norah when she was just a toddler. No older than three. You were away at sea at the time and I thought best not to bother you with it. Do you mind that scruffy ironmonger who lived up the street years ago?'

'Pearson. "Rabbitty" Pearson. He was locked up, wasn't he? I don't think I ever knew what for.'

'Interfering with little girls.'

Joe Moffatt turned to face his wife with sudden attention.

'As I say, Norah was only a toddler. One minute she was playing in the front garden. Next minute she was gone. It was washing day. I was hanging the clothes out the back and when I looked for her in the garden she was gone. The police found her crying in the park and brought her home. A "nasty man" had carried her away, she told them. They said she was unharmed but who can tell? That same week another little girl was taken from her house. Rabitty Pearson was caught and locked up after that and we never saw hair nor hide of him since that day.'

'You should've told me, Edith.'

'While you were at sea I was left to bring up the children on my own and it was sometimes hard to know the right thing to do. Norah seemed all right. A quiet little lass. Never any trouble.'

'So why are you telling me this now?'

'I began to wonder if anything did happen at that time and if it has put her off men for ever.'

'She's got plenty of men friends.'

'Always did have boy friends but the only time she took a husband she left him after the first night.'

'Good job I never knew about this.' Joe's clenched fists stiffened at his side. 'I'd ha' murdered the bastard.'

'She'll never marry. I'm sure of that now. To tell the truth, it's my opinion she never did intend to marry the Russell lad.'

Joe looked at her in astonishment. 'You're a close one and no mistake.'

'That's what I believe.'

'Why would she hide the truth from the Russells?'

'So's not to hurt their feelings. They knew their son wanted to marry her. How would they feel if they knew she had turned him down?'

'So what is she doing out here?'

Edith shrugged. 'Pity to turn down an invitation like this one, especially when she was fed up with England after the war.'

They fell silent, busy with their own thoughts. They stood together on the afterdeck of the ship that was taking them back to their northern hemisphere and watched, with mixed feelings, as the coastline of Australia faded into the distance.

Joe pointed with the stem of his pipe. The creaming furrow of the wake was taking a wide curve. 'She's changing course. Making for home.'

Part Two

Nine

A ndrew dated and signed the last prescription on the pile and put away his pen. The date was significant. 16 October 1960. His birthday. He was forty-four today. Six years to go to his half century. If the next fifty were to be anything like the first then he may as well seek oblivion right now. An extensive pharmacy was at his disposal. Just a joke.

Greeting cards arrived from his father and mother. The twins, Tina and Gwen, never forgot though they were both fully occupied with their children. There was a hand-painted effort from his godson, Philip, and greetings from Simon, lewd as usual. He was back in Berlin after a spell in Cyprus. Recently married, he brought his wife to meet Andrew.

'A bit posh,' he would reply to Norah's query. '"Daddy" is Simon's commanding officer, a terrifying chap with a monocle and a big behind, according to Simon.'

Lord, how he missed Simon. He was like the fizz in tonic and the gin was flat without him.

He gathered up his birthday cards and slipped them out of sight into his briefcase. Forty-four seemed a long stride past forty. Forty still had some spark about it. Forty-four had lost it. By this time most men were launched upon their chosen lifestyle. Not he. He was still marking time, if not actually retreating. What was he waiting for? What was there to wait for?

Five years of what should have been his most productive

period were squandered in the prison camp. He was left with the overwhelming feeling of being cheated of life. Nothing about postwar Britain had come up to his expectations. Nothing had turned out as he had hoped. The girl he had dreamed about during those five barren years in captivity did not want him.

Ah, poor chap.

Self-pity was quickly followed by self-loathing. What was the good of going on like this, a miserable sod who made life joyless not only for himself but for everyone around him.

At one time it would have seemed incredible that he would ever look back on wartime days with anything like nostalgia, but that period spent in hut 6 and the men who shared it with him had acquired a heroic patina over the intervening years. The occasional personality collision faded into the overriding memory of companionship.

He remembered the shared support through the bad times, the laughter through the mad times. He remembered how, at all times, the hope of final victory hung before them, an inextinguishable beacon in the gloom of their everyday existence.

All that was twenty years ago. Different script. Different world now. Even the reunion with his old hut mates five years after their release had fallen flat on its face. Winstanley, the smart character, had sent a message to say he was unavoidably detained in Scotland but, 'Bottoms up, old chaps! Have one for me.'

'He's in the middle of a very messy divorce.' Johnnie Jackson had met him in Waverley Station, Edinburgh. 'Looked a bit careworn, did our Winnie. Not your tricky Dicky any more.'

The bar of a deathly quiet country pub was not the best choice for a reunion of fellows who, since their release, had patently taken on family cares and responsibilities along with extra weight. A lively backdrop of muzak might have helped but, in this silent bar where the only sound was a flustered butterfly beating itself into a coma against a window, every utterance seemed unbelievably vapid, especially when two pairs of ears, those of the barmaid and the village sponger, were determined not to miss a word of the strangers' conversation.

Barney's unidentifiable stews cooked in a tin hat over a primus and the deadly poteen they made out of rotten potatoes kept the reminiscences going for a while. They recalled the blustering Herr Doktor Leutnant Golze and the British corporal, a wizard with electronics, who risked his life every night by tuning into the BBC.

'What was his name again?' How could they have forgotten him?

Captain Barnfather (Retd) laughed more loudly, resurrected more old jokes to fill the listening spaces and called for more beer. But despite the beer, the reunion flattened out and soon they were discussing how to control moss in lawns. Five years of close rewarding friendship were blown away in an afternoon.

'We must do this again,' they said on parting but they all knew this would not happen. The relationship was as cold as yesterday's porridge. Gradually even the contact of Christmas cards dried up. It had always been left to the wives to keep this arrangement working, the exception being Barney's wife. He had married a strong-minded senior administrator in the National Health Service. She bullied him as much as his late mother had done and she had obviously decided, probably with some justification, that her husband's wartime companions were a bad influence upon him. He could write his own Christmas cards.

Of the six who had shared the same hut, only Andrew remained a bachelor and no one had the courage to mention a certain fraulein. There was little about his appearance to suggest he was a happy man.

A knock on his surgery door recalled him from his reverie, back to the present day. The practice receptionist poked her head in. 'That's the last of your patients, Dr Mount. I have filed this morning's records.'

I wonder, Andrew thought, if I told her it was my birthday today would she smile and say 'Happy Birthday'. She never smiles. But then, neither do I. He took his trilby from the hat-stand and went out into the blustery autumn day to buy himself some lunch.

He had declined the responsibility of senior partner in this team of doctors although he had more experience than either of the other two.

'Quiet chap,' they agreed. 'Easy to get on with. Never quite recovered from the war.'

It was a chilly morning. He shrank inside his jacket and wished he was wearing his overcoat. Passers-by leant into the wind, bowed as if by the weight of the heavy sky. The damp and salty air blew straight across the water from Ireland, riming the lips, sneaking cold rivulets inside coat collars. Already there were signs of approaching winter. Yellowing leaves of the chestnut trees, first to come, first to go, drifted down and bowled along the pavements to join the empty cigarette packets and greasy chip papers in sheltered corners. Next thing will be old people slipping on the wet leaves, coming to the surgery with their broken bones.

He took his usual seat by the window in the ABC café. It was steamy-warm in here. The windows ran with condensation but the draught from the door lifted the cocoa-matting and his feet were frozen.

Fish and chips today. Sausage and chips yesterday.

'Tea or coffee?' The waitress, scribbling on her pad, cast about for likely talent at the other tables.

Andrew looked at her empty face with its 'couldn't care less' expression. 'TEA!' he barked and she jumped alert.

With an angry gesture he shoved the brimming ashtray away from him.

'The doc is in a foul mood,' she reported to the kitchen. 'Watch your step, girls.'

Everything about this morning added to the smouldering discontent brought about by his birthday. *I don't have to stay in this dump,* he told himself. *Every boring fruitless day is followed by another of the same. My life has become as aimless as a treadmill.*

By the time he had finished the last greasy, soggy chip Andrew had made up his mind. He had had enough of the uninspiring practice with its varicose veins and its gallbladders. It was time to go. He would speak to the partners this afternoon asking them to release him. He was prepared to work until a replacement could be found, to a limit of three months, preferably less.

'Where are you going, Andrew? This is a sudden decision.'

'Australia,' he said. It was the first place that came into his head but now that he had voiced it the idea seemed admirable. 'To visit a friend.'

Over the years, Dog Creek had prospered. Business was stirring. Farmers were enjoying good prices for wool and meat. Dan and Reg were among those landowners seriously considering the purchase of a small plane to streamline their everyday business activities. All along the roads to Dog Creek and beyond you would hear the jingling of drovers' harnesses and the agitated clattering of the little feet of sheep. Cow pats plastered the bitumen. Cattle, horses and sheep were on the move, to fresh pastures or to the saleyards.

Trade was brisk at the Diggers' and the Loch Lomond garage had taken on an extra hand, a New Australian. That was the name given to the great influx of homeless men and women euphemistically referred to as Displaced Persons who were washed up like driftwood after the tide of war receded in Europe. Australia offered them a new life and called them New Australians.

The man who came to work at the garage was from Latvia originally, a trained locksmith with a thick accent. Stepan, he was called. No one could pronounce his surname. He was forty years old, though from his gaunt face and grey hair you would have thought him to be much older. He didn't say much. That suited Bluey and Pete, who quickly discovered that his clever locksmith fingers translated easily into automobile mechanics. 'He's a good cobber,' they stoutly defended their shy stranger, 'only we can't understand a bloody word he sez.'

Itinerant labourers came to the town seeking work, picking grapes, mending roofs and, at the same time, supporting local businesses. They bought up all the billy-cans in Pa Wilcox's store and drank all the beer in the Diggers'. Commercial travellers came knocking at doors, selling furniture polish, ladies' stockings and bottles of magic hair restorer.

More houses were built. More babies were born. Norah engaged Rose, the younger sister of Mary's Lily, to help in the clinic and taught her basic hygiene and simple treatments. A soft-hearted girl, she was liable to dissolve into tears for any suffering patient. Top Hat was still Norah's Major Domo, irreplaceable as a guard and bouncer even though he still took himself off for unspecified periods of walkabout. Norah understood that he needed to renew contact with the genius of his native land and the allure of its women. He always came back to the clinic no matter how long he was absent.

The sitting room built for Norah by Daddy Watts offered a handy place for a game of cards with the Russell family, a whisky with Dr Jebb after a tiring clinic day.

For him, every clinic day was becoming a tiring day and he liked nothing better after such a day than to put his feet up on Norah's settee, drink her whisky and ask her about

England. He grew maudlin about Soho and the Fitz, neither place meaning anything to north-country Norah.

'Look, Dr Jebb,' she said one evening before his tongue had time to run away with him, 'I think you should advertise for an assistant. There's too much work for one doctor now.'

And Dr Jebb, with reluctance, had to agree. He was feeling his age. 'But it won't be one of those Clever Charlies who know it all,' he warned Norah as his last defence fell. 'He's got to know who's boss.'

His advertisement in the *Sydney Morning Herald* 'Professional Vacancies' column duly appeared and produced one applicant. Dr Jebb had no choice but to engage him. Martin Goodfellow MB BSc was a very earnest young man with a long neck and horn-rimmed spectacles on what, with honesty, could only be described as a beak. 'Dr Emu', Top Hat called him and the soubriquet was apt.

The new doctor was bursting with enthusiasm for the job ahead and positively bounced with delight at the prospect of working in this 'romantic' outpost in the bush.

'Seems keen,' Norah offered.

'Still wet behind the ears,' Jebb grunted. 'He'll learn. Enthusiasm doesn't last out here.' He handed her a bottle of whisky. 'My turn, I think.' Which meant that he would be at liberty to stay behind for a drink after the clinic if and when it suited him.

Reg, adding up his columns of figures in the Wirrawee account books, announced to Dan that the cost of a small plane was quite acceptable and would bring its own rewards by increased efficiency on the station. A good level paddock was tidied up for use as a runway and a rugged Second World War pilot landed the Auster and proceeded to teach Reg how to fly it. Norah's latest letter to Cathy was about this exciting method of travel.

Reg soon got the hang of it. He flies off to Sydney to agricultural conferences so that he can keep up with all the latest farming methods. Marian and I sometimes go with him. We go to a concert or the theatre while he is about his business. He has splashed out on a smart suit and a new akubra. He looks just like your typical prosperous Aussie station owner. I can scarcely tear Marian away from the chic boutiques in Double Bay. She's got a fantastic figure. All the shop assistants love her. They sold her a wonderful slippery green sheath. With her coppery hair she looks stunning. Wait till Reg sees her in it. He'll think he's married a mermaid.

How is your little family? Are you stopping at three or are you aiming to be like the old woman who lived in a shoe? How time flies. Philip will be eleven now and lucky Alison has two big brothers to escort her.

There is some talk of the Shire Authority building me a new clinic. Dog Creek population is increasing all the time. Quite a few refugees from Europe. Australia must seem like paradise to them after the Nazi labour camps. Do you remember Hilde? The Jewish nurse who escaped from Germany? I wonder what became of her. I send my love to you all,

Always your dear friend,
Norah

Ten

O n his next free weekend, Andrew took a train to Euston, then the tube via Liverpool Street to Epping, the latest address for Cathy and Ray. They had moved to a bigger house and garden to accommodate their growing family. As with the previous address there was easy access to the shipping heart of London. Ray was rising steadily up the ladder of seniority in the shipping line which served Australia and New Zealand.

Andrew was always assured of a warm welcome here. Once inside Cathy's kitchen with its stews and puddings to tease the nose, paints and crayons and children at the table and Ray reaching for the corkscrew, he could unwind.

Philip, his godson, was a serious-minded little boy. His younger brother, Michael, was more like his mother, a child of inventions and enthusiasms. Their sister Alison at four was generally accepted to be a handful. Some people went further and described her as a little horror.

Over tea Andrew told them of his plans to visit Australia.

Cathy squealed with delight. 'To see Norah!'

'Hopefully, and perhaps to find a job there for a while. I'd like to have a spell out of England and I've come to ask your help, Ray. You once told me that there was always room for a doctor on your freighters as an extra numerary for the voyage. Is this still the case and, if so, do I qualify?'

'No problem there, old chap. What's brought on this sudden decision?'

'I'm stale, fed up and forty-four. I need to get out. Anywhere in the world would do but the fact that Norah is in Australia makes that an attractive destination.'

'Does she know?'

'I'll write as soon as I find a ship willing to sign me on.'

'In the beginning it was to be a two-year stay for Norah,' Cathy sighed. 'It's twelve years since she left. She hasn't even met her godson.'

Alison lifted her eyes from the Plasticine cow she was making. 'And she hasn't met me,' she reminded them sternly.

Cathy wrote to Norah. 'He's finally decided to quit that country practice in Cumbria and join the real world again. See if you can cheer him up and then maybe, when he comes home, you will come with him? We still miss you dreadfully, dear Norah. Always will. The children think that Auntie Norah is make-believe.'

As she licked the envelope flap she thought ruefully, *But you don't miss us, my dear. You've got your Marian now.*

Here on the Wirrawee verandah the temperature was 90 degrees Fahrenheit with 92 per cent humidity. Norah's bare feet sought a cool spot on the linoleum floor covering. The Russell family, in which Norah was included as a matter of course, was cooling off after a Christmas dinner of roast goose stuffed with apple, sage and onions and a pudding reeking with brandy.

Reg came from the kitchen with a jug of cold beer. 'Try a drop of ice-cold Australian beer, Norah. They tell me the beer in England is warm!'

Dan roused himself from a post-prandial nap. 'Y'd not want to be drinking cold beer when the temperature is a degree or two below freezing, Reg. Am I right, Norah?'

'Absolutely, Dan. They'll be wearing their winter wool-
lies at home now. Dad will be carrying logs, filling the
coal scuttles. The ground will be hard with frost and he'll
scarcely be able to dig up the potatoes. Not the weather for
ice-cold beer.'

'Your friend will be glad of it on a sticky night like this.'
Norah had just told them the news that Andrew was planning
to visit Australia.

'This is the doctor who was taken prisoner at Dunkirk,
Dad,' Marian explained, 'and spent the rest of the war in
a POW camp.'

'I'll look forward to meeting him. He did his bit, that's
for sure.'

'He'll be welcome here,' said Mary, 'any time.'

'I have known Andrew for ages,' said Norah. 'Captain
of the local cricket team before the war. Cathy says he is
browned off with his little country practice in the north of
England and decided to do a bit of travelling. He's working
his passage on a freighter as ship's doctor.'

'If he docks at Sydney, Reg will fly you down to meet
him, won't you, Reg?' Marian was already hatching plans
for Andrew's entertainment.

'Sure thing.'

Facing the little party on the verandah the setting sun
threw the black mass of the mountain in sharp relief.

'It'll be a good day tomorrow, Norah. Shall we take a
ride to the back blocks?'

Norah nodded. 'OK. I wonder if Andrew rides.'

'I never knew a man who couldn't,' said Reg.

As daylight faded, cooling breezes crept over the land,
came whispering at the verandah screens and drifting
through a house that creaked as it cooled. Dan picked up
his fiddle.

'Is there a drop of Irish whisky left in the cask, Reg?
I've a mind to hear an old tune my father used to play

on Christmas night when he was well topped up with the Irish elixir.'

'"Danny Boy",' Mary urged. 'Yes, please.'

'That old tear-jerker,' Marian sighed.

'I like a good cry,' Mary insisted. 'Especially when I'm happy.'

The next morning, long before the day had time to warm up, Marian and Norah were on their planned ride over the ridge. The dew was heavy on the hillsides, the sheep quietly grazing, the countryside around them unspoilt. Norah tried to imagine the scene through Andrew's eyes. Some twelve years had passed since she last saw him. The Andrew she used to know was probably as changed as she knew herself to be.

It was as though Marian was reading her thoughts. 'I expect you're longing to see Andrew after all this time?'

'He's not essential to my wellbeing, Marian, but of course I am dead keen to show him around this perfect paradise I have found through you.'

After breakfast at the homestead Norah made her way to the clinic where several long-faced men from the village awaited her. There had been a brawl at the Diggers' the previous night. Some cracked heads and broken noses awaited her attention.

Marian spent the afternoon helping her mother to polish and put away in cotton bags the silver cutlery used for the Christmas dinner.

'Pity we don't use it more often, Ma. It is so elegant.'

'It's an heirloom,' said Mary. 'Only for special occasions. I remember having to polish it as a child and I aim to keep it looking just like this for the next occasion we have for celebrating.'

Marian squinted sideways at her mother. 'What are you plotting?'

'Not plotting anything at all,' Mary was quick to excuse

herself. 'But I was wondering – this friend of Norah's who's coming to visit, is he an admirer of hers do you think?'

Marian shrugged. 'We'll have to wait and see. She mentions him from time to time. They trained at the same hospital.'

They polished in silence for a while till Mary, revealing her train of thought said, 'He may be married, of course.'

'I don't think so. Norah told me that he fell in love with a Jewish refugee from Germany years ago. She turned him down and he hasn't looked at another woman since.'

'Time he did,' Mary said firmly. 'And Norah would be a treasure for any man.'

'I don't think she wants to get married, Mother. It's not for the want of suitors. There are graziers round here, widowers and younger blokes as well, who've tried their luck but she keeps 'em all at arm's length. Don't leave the silver out on the off chance of a wedding.'

The SS *Nevis* sailed from Liverpool on 10 January 1961 bound for Australia with a cargo of tractors, engine parts and farm implements which would be exchanged for wool, fruit and meat on the return journey. Andrew sailed with her as ship's doctor.

There had been some explaining to do when he broke the news to his mother that he was about to throw in his job at the Ambleside practice and visit Australia. His father welcomed this initiative from a son who, it seemed, had lost his way in the postwar years. 'Grand chaps, the Australians,' he encouraged Andrew. 'Good soldiers. Fought alongside some of them in the 14–18 war.'

His mother was close to tears. She had wept into her pillow when he was taken prisoner at Dunkirk, wept with joy when he came home at the end of the war and now must weep again. Her only son, her firstborn, handsome, clever, full of promise as a young man but almost a stranger now, was planning to go to the other side of the world. She was sixty-eight years old and in poor health. She might not see him again.

His father came to Tilbury to see him off wearing his Number One Stiff Upper Lip. 'Don't worry about your mother, son, (for they had left her in tears). 'She's got her grandchildren to occupy her.' He gripped his son's shoulder, had to reach for it these days. 'Just keep the letters coming, old boy. Women – you know.' And he walked off the quay before the last goodbye. The leavetaking was painful for all of them, for Andrew as much as for his parents. He was keenly aware that, despite their love, he was a great disappointment to them. He was a disappointment to himself, come to that.

His cabin was small but adequate with a shower, hanging space and capacious drawers under his boxed-in bunk. A bulkhead fitting secured his medical reference books against the rolling of the ship. He unpacked the family photograph of his parents and his sisters and poured himself a double whisky to celebrate this step into an unknown future.

His duties at sea were to conduct a daily sick parade and deal with any injuries. He sent up a private prayer that nothing wildly original would present itself to confound him. Six weeks stretched ahead of him with ports of call on the way for cargo and bunkering before reaching Melbourne and Sydney.

Norah had written to say she would meet him when he docked. He had not seen her since that chill February day in 1949, twelve years ago when she set sail for Australia. To judge from her letters, it would seem that the life suited her, that she had made many friends. He hoped to spend some time with her, before moving on. That, for the time being, was as far as his planning went.

The way ahead was uncluttered, unmarked with old experiences. 'Steady as she goes' was the message from the bridge to the engine room as the *Nevis* confidently dipped her prow into the wintry coastal waters. 'Steady as she goes' was an apt directive for Andrew, too.

He spent his first days at sea familiarizing himself with the available medical equipment and making himself known to the crew. By the time the ship rounded the west point of Spain he had settled into the ship's routine, adjusting easily to this working model of ordered industry and traditional skills.

After dinner in the evening he joined those officers who were not on watch for a relaxing hour or two in the saloon, a cosy, softly lit place where the sea in all its moods could be forgotten for a while; where men far from home and family shared reminiscences and told impossible yarns, some of them true. Duty-free liquor was temptingly cheap but Andrew, reminding himself that a ship's doctor was always on watch, exercised admirable restraint, an action that was not lost on the captain whose bright and beady eye missed not a thing.

The captain was a man of much experience, having joined the line as a deck cadet and worked up the grades to be Master. He ran a disciplined ship. His authority was unquestioned, his responsibilities manifold.

Men at sea learn early not to ask personal questions. Andrew was accepted and respected as a conscientious doctor. That was all that was required of him. Any misgivings he might have had about breaking the old mould of his life evaporated in the company of these strongly individual personalities who had chosen to make the sea their career, who kept the ship safe and in good trim, the navigators and engineers, electricians and radio operators, refrigerating experts, rope makers, carpenters, painters, chartmakers, cooks.

Andrew's responsibility was to keep them all fit for work, a service which earned him a free passage. Money for old rope, he told himself. By the time they berthed in Las Palmas his only casualty had been 'Chippy' who missed his aim with a hammer and fractured his thumb.

As the *Nevis* neared the Equator temperatures soared, but at a speed of 22 knots the ship made her own breeze, providing some comfort for those on board. Andrew and the sixteen-year-old pantry boy, the two uninitiated in the ceremony of 'crossing the line', were thrown fully clothed into the ship's swimming pool, all in good fun until Andrew realized the boy could not swim.

'Don't worry yourself, Doc' he was assured by the crew as he fished the badly scared boy out of the water. 'We're ready with a life belt. Now mebbes the little beggar will learn to swim.'

A hard school, Andrew thought, but the lessons were lifesavers.

Days at sea passed pleasantly for him, identifying passing ships and migrating birds, watching the ever-changing nature of the seas and the skies, all things new to a country doctor.

Shipping increased as they neared the Cape, traders in timber, wine and fruit. He went ashore at Cape Town and would have joined a party setting out to climb Table Mountain, but a certain internal discomfort which he could not account for persuaded him to restrict his explorations to a stroll around the town's markets.

After Cape Town the *Nevis* broke away from a convoy of tankers heading for the Middle East to follow her own course to Australia, across the lonely, the notoriously fickle-tempered Southern Ocean, below the 'roaring forties', in the territory of the enigmatic albatross and the playful dolphin. The *Nevis* was on her own now.

Andrew watched from the foc'sle as the ship's prow, in the manner of a land plough, turned back huge volumes of deep blue water cresting with crystal, casting before her glittering shawls of flying fish. A beautiful ocean, a sapphire sea, he was thinking, but a lonely one. Not to be trusted, some of the sailors said. Many a stout crewman confessed to wearing a rabbit's foot beneath his shirt. He would laugh at his foolishness, of course, but 'You never know with that sea. All smiles one minute and a right bitch the next.'

Despite his very real interest in his surroundings Andrew was conscious of a growing anxiety preying on his mind. The internal discomfort which made itself felt in Cape Town had never left him. In fact it was now developing into a full-blown pain which was becoming increasingly difficult to contain. Desperately he sought palliatives, needing progressively stronger painkillers to help him through his duties.

His eye swept the great watery wastes. As far as the distant horizons, no ship was to be seen, no glimpse of land. Antarctica, the nearest landfall, was many nautical miles away. This was neither the time nor the place for a ship's doctor to go sick, especially when, though he did not then know it, the Southern Ocean was about to live up to its wicked reputation for bad weather.

Eleven

None of the crew showed surprise when the blue of the sea turned to dark grey. The radio officer forecast heavy weather. The barometer took a dive and, as if by a prearranged signal, stormy petrels, those harbingers of storms known to sailors the world over as Mother Carey's Chickens, appeared, weaving and winding over the suddenly turbulent wake of the ship. Dead ahead, malevolent black clouds, hanging low in a sulphur sky, began to roll over the water towards the ship. No sun now. Dark as night, though the clock in the saloon showed midday. Stewards hastened to fit the fiddles around the dining tables and damped down the tablecloths to prevent crockery from sliding on to the deck. By that afternoon the ship was in the grip of a force 9 gale.

Andrew had never imagined such a sea. Through the porthole in his cabin he glimpsed bottomless troughs of boiling gunmetal water erupting in mountainous spouts of green water peaking in foam. Had he not been in pain he could have rejoiced in the majesty of the storm. As it was, every fresh lurch of the ship tore at his gut.

The ship's course took her straight into the heart of the gale. Violent pitching followed by deep rolls athwart the waves threw men off balance and there were injuries needing medical attention. The chef scalded his arm with boiling soup, and the young pantry boy injured his knee. The second officer knocked himself out with a blow against

96

a bulkhead and all the time, as Andrew treated their injuries, he was sickeningly aware that his own symptoms were entirely consistent with a diagnosis of appendicitis.

At last, the fact that the doctor was ill could not be concealed. Following established procedure, the captain radioed head office in England for instructions. These were brief. He was to make for the nearest landfall and put the doctor ashore.

The nearest land was Heard Island in the Antarctic, latitude 58 degrees. In terrible weather conditions the captain stoically attempted to carry out these instructions only to find that Heard Island was locked in ice. There was no way that the doctor could be put ashore. Even if the inhabitants of the island could reach him over the packed ice he would be unlikely to survive the hazardous journey to safety.

The captain took the matter into his own hands and wired London. 'Impossible to land doctor. Heard Island ice-bound. Am making for Melbourne with all speed.'

Andrew voiced his full approval although he was aware that his chances of survival were small if his appendix should rupture. Melbourne was four sailing days away; meanwhile the foul infection within him was approaching a crisis. Without surgical intervention to remove it, the appendix would surely rupture and potentially fatal peritonitis would follow. With the infection threatening to overwhelm his body his fevered brain sought a way out of his predicament. He had already considered the option of operating upon himself and had rejected it as impractical.

As the ship changed course for Melbourne she slammed down on the rollers and slewed in the valleys sending men scudding across the wet decks, clutching at supports. But for the pillows wedging Andrew in his bunk he would have been thrown out. The whole ship's company knew that the doc was perilously ill. Their faces were solemn as

97

they went about their duties. Andrew was a popular figure amongst them.

He cursed malicious Fate which tracked him down wherever he was. There was no hiding place. There was never to be any lasting happiness for him. *Is it all to end like this?* teeth clenched in pain, he demanded of his God who knew no mercy. *To die of appendicitis halfway to Australia? Am I not to be given another chance?*

Perhaps Andrew's desperate call was heard. Perhaps mischievous Fate suddenly tired of its bullying ways. Like a shaft of light an idea took shape in his mind. A remote possibility occurred to him that if he could lower the temperature of his body almost to freezing he might delay, even arrest, the onset of peritonitis. Frozen cells could not reproduce themselves. He called for the refrigerating engineer. 'Keep me packed in ice, Mac. Keep me cold as a frozen kipper till we reach Melbourne, even if I am too cold to speak, just keep piling on the ice.'

It was a long chance but it was the only chance. As the violence of the storm abated. Andrew considered his situation. He felt extremely ill. He had a raging temperature and was drifting off into unconsciousness from time to time. After all, he told himself resignedly in lucid moments, he would be no great loss to anyone if he died. He could have died at Dunkirk or in the POW camp in Poland and, when Hilde turned him down, he could have taken an overdose. It had been a considered option. None of these things had happened. Looking at it like that he had been given an extension of his life and if it were to run out now, so be it.

He ate nothing at all during those last traumatic days in order to rest his gut, relying solely on water to keep himself alive. Mac, with his bucket of ice, scarcely left his side. They were still two days from Melbourne when the appendix perforated. Andrew felt the small implosion and the stab of excruciating pain. *This is it*, he thought. Ragged scraps of memory flicked through his mind before he sank into unconsciousness, the proud, dark head of the woman he loved, the anxious face of his mother, his good friend, Simon.

On the following day he found he was still alive. A cold hand was laid on his forehead.

'Cripes, Doc, I thought you'd hopped it.'

News of the ship's crisis had spread by telegraph to Australia. When the captain dropped anchor in Melbourne harbour there was an ambulance waiting to take Andrew to hospital, more dead than alive. Headlines were already spread across the newspapers. 'Pommie Doc freezes himself to keep alive.' 'Life and death race from the Antarctic.'

Surgeons found that the appendix had indeed ruptured but, because of the low body temperature, peritonitis had been confined to a small area of the abdominal cavity. The refrigerating engineer had stuck to his job even though it had seemed to him that all was lost. Andrew's condition was critical but there was at least a chance that he might survive.

Norah's newspaper always arrived a day late, courtesy of the Wilcox family who ran a delivery service from the railway halt at Coonaban, twenty miles north-west of Dog Creek. Her heart leapt into her mouth when she saw the headlines in the *Sydney Morning Herald.*

'I've got to go, Marian. Straight away.'

Reg was already pulling on his boots. 'Grab your swag, girl. Whatever you need to take with you. I'll fly you to Sydney airport. You'll get a connection to Melbourne there.'

Marian's hand on her arm stilled the rising panic. 'I'll tell Graham. Mum and I will help out at the clinic in the meantime. Go and see to your friend. Nothing else matters.'

Norah handed over the essential keys. 'The only medicines Rose has access to are cascara and magnesia. She can't do any damage with those. She can treat Billy Kehoe's knee and Grandma Wilcox's ulcer. She's a sensible girl.'

'Like her sister Lily, and we will lend a hand.'

'Oh, Marian.'

Marian saw tears threatening as Norah embraced her. 'Off you go. Reg is waiting.'

The news spread throughout the settlement that the doctor who'd been in the papers, who'd frozen himself to keep alive, was Sister Norah's friend from England. Everyone wanted to help including Dr Jebb whose professional interest was aroused by this doctor's do-it-yourself treatment for a perforated appendix.

They landed on the private strip at Sydney's Mascot Airport. Reg carried her bag to the check-in. He put a hand lightly on her shoulder. 'Keep us in the know, Norah. We're here to help.'

Unprepared for the toll exacted by the severe infection Andrew had sustained, Norah experienced a moment of indecision in recognizing him when she was shown to his bed. His light-coloured hair, which had receded since she last saw him, gave him an unnaturally high forehead. His face was thin and pale as bone. His half-closed eyes, which had not yet registered her presence, were sunk in dark hollows. Deeply disturbed by his appearance, she gently took his limp hand in hers.

His eyes flickered open and the blank gaze warmed. His faint smile, his whispered 'Darling Norah' brought tears to her eyes.

She bent low. 'I am staying here with you, Andy, until you are fit to travel and then I'll take you home with me. I will look after you.'

He nodded, seeking no part in the decision-making. She

ran a hand over his forehead. It was damp and clammy cold. His hair was stringy with sweat. She had been relieved to learn that he was now off the danger list. Nevertheless it was patently obvious that he was still a very sick man.

'I damn near kicked the bucket, old girl.' His voice was a thread. He had neither air nor energy for further effort.

She rose from the bedside chair. 'I am going to have a word with your doctor. I'll be back.'

A week passed before he could be moved and then only because Norah was qualified to look after him. He was growing a little stronger every day and made an attempt at a joke when the refrigerating engineer, along with others of the crew, came to pay him a farewell visit before they sailed.

'Lucky we never ran out of ice, Mac. I'd have been a very dead doc without your help.'

Sandy MacGregor, a short, unassuming man, swelled to six feet tall at this simple truth. Future shipmates would talk about him in the saloons of ships at sea. 'Did you ever know a Freezer by the name of Sandy MacGregor?'

Most would have heard of him but the tale would be told again.

When Andrew was able to be moved a medical airlift was provided to fly him with Norah as escort to Ironstone emergency air strip where Reg and Marian waited to drive them to Dog Creek. A room at Wirrawee had been offered for his convalescence but Norah would not let him out of her sight. He would stay with her until he was truly restored to health. Marian and Rose had prepared her bedroom for him and put up a makeshift stretcher for her on the verandah. By the time he was helped from the car and into bed he was exhausted. Too tired to speak, he lay back against the cool pillows and closed his eyes. Through the open window came the perfumes of the bush and the ticky-tacky pecking noises of foraging wagtails. Andrew slept.

Evening sunlight slanting into the room lit upon a tall jar of crimson waratahs picked by Rose. 'Make sick fella good again.'

Norah took her hand. 'Good girl, Rose.'

They quietly withdrew, Rose to tell Top Hat of the new arrival, Marian and Norah to the sitting room with a pot of tea.

'You're not bothered about the tittle-tattle, Norah?'

'What do you mean?' Norah's puzzlement was genuine.

Marian laughed. 'You are the giddy limit. For a very proper English lady you don't give a damn about proprieties. I mean that you and your smashing doctor are living together. That'll set the tongues wagging!'

'How ridiculous,' Norah said crossly. 'Andrew and I are old friends. Known each other for donkeys' years. He's like a brother to me.'

She wrote to Cathy that night and told her the whole story.

> He's making progress now but he's terribly weak. Marian and I will look after him and Doctor Jebb is a good doctor when he's not on the whisky.
>
> If you are in touch with any of the others please ask them to write to him, especially Simon, but then, I don't suppose you hear from him.

'A little dig at the end,' mused Cathy. 'She hasn't forgiven me for marrying Ray instead of her blue-eyed boy.'

Twelve

Once recovered from the journey, Andrew rallied considerably and began to take an interest in his surroundings. Marian was a frequent visitor, sitting with him when Norah was called away. He enjoyed her company and the picture she conjured up of life at Wirrawee; of the brumbies she was breaking in, of Reg's new dam and her stories of the aboriginal children at the creek. In answer to his casual enquiry, did she have any children of her own, she gave a brief, 'Nope. Didn't happen.' And changed the subject.

'As soon as you're fit you must come and visit us at Wirrawee. My mother is anxious to meet you but does not want to tire you until you are well enough. She doesn't get about much now. Arthritis.'

She chattered and clattered about the sick room, which was Norah's bedroom, in her good leather boots, wagging her aggressive little bottom in its tight jodhpurs. The room was too small to contain her energy. What furniture there was seemed to be continually in her way. Andrew learned to shut his eyes before the crash. With her downy tanned arms and cropped hair the colour of beech leaves in autumn she was like a restless nut-brown animal in an alien environment. It was 'Oh, sorry, sorry!' as she bumped into his bed, spilt the water in his jug, tripped over his slippers. 'I'm better with horses, you see,' she explained as she tried to heave him up the bed with little success.

She amused him but it was Norah who knew how to make

him comfortable. Neither felt any embarrassment over these attentions. She was still an attractive woman, though she must be over forty now. Years ago he became aware of a physical barrier surrounding Norah and so, when she leaned close to him and washed the bits he could not reach, he saw only professional care in her eyes. Her devotion to his comfort touched him deeply.

'I'm a lucky chap to have two beautiful nurses to look after me.'

'We're both beautiful,' Marian happily agreed, 'but only one of us is a nurse.' She flopped down on his bed with a bounce that made him wince. The operation site was still tender. 'I'm the maid-of-all-work.'

Letters came from his family thanking Norah for her care of Andrew, and a case of champagne from Simon now serving in Cyprus. Cathy's instructions were to 'Do exactly as Norah tells you, Andy dear. You are the patient this time.'

Absently, Andrew fingered the pages of Cathy's letter. He was about to break his self-imposed rule, learned in the hard school of a Polish Oflag, never to ask personal questions.

'Don't you miss Cathy, Norah?'

'I did at first. Still do, actually,' Norah confessed. 'Even after all these years.'

'I could never understand why you had to cut away to the other side of the world, breaking up your long friendship. You say you miss her? Believe, me, Norah, she misses you.'

'She's got Ray.'

'Can't she have you as well?'

Norah looked uncomfortable.

'Are you not prepared to share Cathy with anyone?' softly Andrew turned the point of the knife.

Norah coloured. For a moment it seemed she was about to make an angry response, then thought better of it. 'That's a sore spot, Andrew. Don't touch it.'

Instantly contrite, he stretched out a hand. 'Forgive me. That was unkind.'

The flush on her cheek died away as quickly as it had arisen. 'That's all right,' she said with sudden weariness. 'You just happen to have hit the nail on the head. And I am ashamed. But she is my Cathy and I'll not share her, not with an ex-patient with a history of tuberculosis while our own dear Simon is sent off with his tail between his legs.'

'I know all about jealousy,' Andrew said quietly. 'And I know it is self-destructive. A close brush with Infinity, however, such as I experienced on the ship, concentrates the mind wonderfully, throwing up images of yourself that are not particularly palatable. I saw the bald truth. I was like an apple with a beastly worm at work inside. I recognized that worm. Its name is jealousy and it has been gnawing at me since the end of the war. I don't need to remind you of Hilde.' He laid aside the letters and settled back on his pillows, wearied by all the talking. 'I have now excised the worm, Norah. Straightforward wormectomy.'

Norah smiled fondly at him. 'Let me rearrange your pillows so you can have a nap.' Before she left him she turned at the door. 'I think I would need an outsize worm pill before I'd be eligible to join your club.'

'It's up to you.'

When the crisis in Cyprus died down, Simon, now Colonel Poole, was posted once more to Germany, this time with comfortable accommodation for himself and his family near the town of Celle. He was having breakfast. His wife, Lorna, was in the act of pouring his tea when she was arrested by the concern on his face when he read a letter from his father.

'Something wrong?'

'Cyril Lewis is dead. 'Flu.' He did not even look up.

'Cathy's father,' she said (as if he didn't know). She passed his teacup.

Simon looked at his watch, tucked the letter in his trouser pocket and got to his feet. 'Funeral tomorrow.' He blew on his tea to cool it and drank it in a gulp. 'Got to go, dear. Do you mind? Pay my respects. A wartime mate of my father's. Home Guard. I'll get a twenty-four-hour pass and be back tomorrow night.'

She nodded, not particularly pleased but prepared to be obliging. 'I know you thought a lot of him.'

Simon turned to the two children eating their way through plates of cornflakes. 'Now you two monkeys are to look after Mummy while I'm away and be very good or there'll be no presents when I come back.'

'You'll be seeing your parents, Simon? Give them my best wishes.' *And, of course*, Lorna added to herself, *he'll see Cathy. But that was schoolboy love. Before he met me.* She put up her face to be kissed. 'I might pick up Verity and do a little shopping.' Her price for being wifely.

The cemetery on the hill overlooking the sea at Eastport Bay was unprotected from a bleak and salty wind that snatched the dribble from a leaking stand-tap and spewed it horizontal over sodden ground, hurled great gusts at the cringing tombstones, whipped the black skirts of the women, wrestled with their hats.

Four women stood at the open grave. Simon, standing a little way apart from the rest of the mourners, recognized Mrs Lewis, with the blank face of a sleepwalker, supported by one of Cathy's sisters. Another sister stood huddled against her husband, her face buried in a handkerchief. The third and smallest of the three sisters was Cathy.

Simon drank in every detail of her like blotting paper on spilt ink. For so many years he had held back from any possibility of seeing her once she became wife to someone else. Now he was galloping back through the years to the wild, fun-loving girl with the freckled face and cheeky turned-up nose, to the nurse in battledress in the North African desert hospitals and now, here she was, older and chubbier but still the essential Cathy, standing by the open grave of her father.

Stiff and straight she stood as if for the National Anthem, uncaring of the rain and the wind. Simon hoped never again to see a face as sad as hers beneath its little black hat. Cathy had adored her father.

Her black shoes were caked in yellow clay. Rivulets of yellow mud ran at her feet down into the hole where they had lowered her father in his shiny new oak coffin with brass handles.

The urge to go to her side was almost overpowering. He pulled back, reminding himself that she was not his to comfort. She belonged to somebody else.

The minister presiding lifted his voice to be heard against the roar of the sea and the wind. His black cassock swirled in wicked dance about his irreligious boots and lifted his careful hair to give the game away.

The first clods landed with a thump and the waiting friends melted away to partake of sherry and biscuits at the house where Cyril Lewis used to live. There were curious glances at the army officer standing alone and the whisper went round. 'Cathy's old flame.' Cathy was the last to leave the heaped-up earth which marked her father's resting place.

Simon had not intended to make his presence known. He had come to pay his personal tribute to Cathy's father for whom he had always felt the greatest respect. That done, there was no need for him to stay longer. Prudence urged him to take himself off for his own peace of mind.

He waited for her because he could do no other.

'Cathy.'

She raised red-rimmed eyes to take in Simon's presence, this tall, imposing army officer in his British warm, wearing the insignia of colonel on his shoulder and pleading in his eyes. She managed a wavering smile. 'You look like a golden labrador in that coat.'

Then the tears started again. 'Oh, Simon. I loved my dad.'

'I know. I had to come, Cathy. I greatly admired your father.' He took her arm. She was smaller than he remembered, compared with Lorna, and hastily banished all such comparisons. 'Come on. I'll take you home. I must speak to your mother, though I have nothing to say.'

She felt the strength of him and leaned on him.

At the airport he picked up some colouring books for the children and a copy of the *Ideal Home* for Lorna then flew back to Germany.

That is all that happened between them, Simon and Cathy, after a long, long separation, but in some extraordinary fashion it seemed to both of them that this was the right way to acknowledge and accept their chosen paths.

Simon wrote about this to Andrew and Norah. *'Mr Lewis was just one of the many deaths following the flu epidemic this year. Norah will know how devastated Cathy is.'*

Andrew passed Simon's letter to Norah.

'She will be heartbroken,' Norah agreed. 'She and her dad were great pals. He was always interested in Cathy's friends and concerned about what became of us all. Simon went to the funeral for all of us, really.'

'I'm glad they were able to meet again, after so many years.'

'I wonder if they found each other much changed.'

'Simon still looks like a rugby full-back and he sports a splendid moustache.'

Norah laughed. 'I remember he promised Cathy years

ago that he would one day be a brigadier with a plume of whiskers.'

Andrew smiled. 'I'd say he's on the way. He's got the whiskers. The brigadier is within reach if he doesn't get retired before that.'

Thirteen

As soon as he felt well enough Andrew insisted that Norah should reclaim her bedroom and he took over the camp bed on the verandah. It was springtime in Norah's garden. Bird-watching had never been a hobby of his but now he began to identify the cheeky willie wagtails and perky crested bul-buls, the noisy minah and flocks of tiny honey-eaters who descended on the creamy blossom of the gum trees, rattling the brittle leaves into a frenzy as they probed for nectar.

During the day passers-by on their way to the store or the pub would stop to have a crack with the Pommie doc, to their mutual entertainment. Dr Jebb was a frequent caller, delighting in recounting the tales of his misspent youth while in London prior to taking his Fellowship in surgery.

'Spent most of my money and sowed some wild oats there,' he would expand, in enjoyable recall. 'The Fitzroy Tavern in Soho, that was the place to be in the 1930s. Artists and poets, drunks and prostitutes and a smattering of geniuses; Salvation Army sheilas in bonnets and bows selling the *War Cry* to Spanish revolutionists and communists alike, wine-ohs and down-and-outs. You'd find them all in the Fitz. For me it was an experience of more value than any FRCS.'

Dr Jebb's appearance was not what Andrew had expected of a senior medical practitioner. His light-coloured safari jacket carried reminders of an earlier curry supper. A spotted

110

cravat which had seen better days attempted to hide the fact that there was no possibility of his collar closing and a belt of kangaroo leather slung sub-paunch deceived no one but himself in its tally of notches. Aboriginal washerwomen were constantly coming and going at his modest establishment in Ironstone but none of them cared enough about their employer to keep him well turned out.

He took a paternal interest in Andrew's welfare, however. 'Soon as you're fit, get yourself down to Sydney, the big smoke. It's a great swinging city these days. You should see the opera house we're building. It's an eye-opener. I can give you an introduction to the medical fraternity. Put you up for my club if you like?'

Andrew demurred. 'Later perhaps, but not just yet. I love the peace of this place. I'd like to stay awhile here although I can't go on indefinitely sponging on Norah's hospitality. I will have to stir myself and earn a living sometime. Right now I don't feel like anything more strenuous than a game of cards.'

Out came the well thumbed pack from the doctor's safari jacket. 'You're on. What's the stakes?'

The evenings passed pleasantly, with Marian and Reg dropping in for a gin and a round of poker. It was easy for Andrew to think that he could continue in this irresponsible vein for ever. The very modest household expenses were shared between himself and Norah. Meat was cheap. There was a whole sheep in the Wirrawee freezer which Andrew had won off Reg at pontoon. Locally grown vegetables and fruit were plentiful and cheap Australian wine was moving up-market all the time.

The building of the new clinic had begun and Andrew could make himself useful during the transition from out-dated facilities to a smart modern building with space for up-to-date appliances. The old now discarded clinic continued to lean drunkenly against Norah's living space but

111

she had some as yet unformed plan to buy the whole building from the Shire Health Authority if the price was right.

'They can't expect much for it,' she confided to Andrew. 'And Daddy Watts could make a good job of the conversion.'

Andrew was impressed. 'If he knocks down the internal walls that would give you a lot more room.' The project began to assume the look of the possible.

There was little for Norah to spend her salary on in Dog Creek and trips to Sydney were rare. She imagined her savings would be adequate for a modest outlay.

Andrew was now a frequent visitor to Wirrawee. While Norah and Marian exercised the horses he made himself familiar with this considerable estate run so efficiently by Dan and Reg. With the help of a jobber from the town, they were building a new cow shed and installing electric fences. Andrew offered help but could not match their skills. He watched as Reg put a flock of panicky sheep through a cleansing dip, handling rams as if they were kittens.

Compliments made Reg uneasy. 'It's my job,' he said. 'Reckon I'd make a mess of taking out a pair of tonsils.'

Over many a cup of tea Andrew sat with Mary on the verandah, listening to tales of her girlhood in Shingles Post further north and how Dan brought her to his parents' home at Wirrawee.

'And I've been here ever since,' she would say with perfect equanimity, 'and ask no more of the dear Lord than to let me die here. But not before my Dan. He'll never remember to change his shirt without me there to remind him.'

And then she would fall back on the ever-present grief which would never leave her. 'But for the wretched war Keith would have been here today, his wife at his side, his children playing in the field out there.'

'His wife?'

'Norah, of course. Didn't she tell you?'

'I didn't realize—' Andrew began. 'I knew they had met during the war. I didn't know how serious it was.'

Mary nodded. 'They were very much in love. He wrote saying he had found the girl he wanted to marry and the next news we received was that he had been killed while fighting the Japanese in New Guinea. Norah is very loyal to his memory. There are plenty men round here who would jump at the chance of slipping a ring on her finger but she has never encouraged any of them.'

No, thought Andrew, *and I don't suppose she ever will. She doesn't want a husband. All she wants is a big brother. He sighed inwardly. I could have told you that years ago, dear Mrs Russell.*

'She made a good job of you when you were so ill,' Mary turned her attention to this very eligible bachelor tucking into her Dundee cake. 'You were in a bad way when Norah brought you from the Melbourne hospital.'

'I'm indebted to Norah. And Marian too. I will be sad to leave them but I will have to move on soon. My bank manager suggests I should start to earn a living once more.'

When the time was right the job simply fell into his lap.

It was Graham Jebb who came up with the idea. The practice had been growing alarmingly during the last few years. 'Folks keep having babies and at the same time are intolerably lax about shrugging off the mortal coil. I had to employ an assistant a year ago. You've met him, chap called Goodfellow. I can't get round the back blocks like I used to and this character does some of the longer drives and night calls. Stroppy young puppy. Thinks he knows it all, of course.'

'I have met him,' said Andrew. 'He came to the clinic once seeking plaster of Paris.'

113

'No experience to speak of, but he'll learn and that is where you come in. He wants to go to England to take his FRCS next year, like I did. But I'll need to find a locum to take his place while he's overseas. Do you fancy taking it on? For part of the time, if you don't want to commit yourself to a longer spell.' His crabby fingers rattled through a nervous arpeggio on the table top between them. 'Share cases with me, take on some of the longer drives.' Persuasive, he was, and a little bit sorry for himself. 'This damn gout gives me hell from time to time.'

Andrew was not enthusiastic, not at all confident that his medical experience would cover emergencies peculiar to the outback of Australia. 'This is a very different practice from my previous one in the English Lake District.'

Confident now of winning the argument, Jebb puffed happily on his pipe. 'Your friend Norah will keep you right. Regulation remuneration, of course. And you could take over Goodfellow's accommodation in Ironstone – but maybe you'd prefer to carry on here?' suddenly uncharacteristically sensitive.

'No. I have trespassed on Norah's hospitality too long already. If I decide to take the job, I'll probably go for Goodfellow's accommodation.'

'She's a fine woman, your Norah.'

Andrew was amused at the naïve approach to a question which he knew was teasing the doctor and resolved to put him out of his misery. 'She's not my woman. She's not anyone's woman. She's not the marrying kind.'

Jebb cocked a quizzical eye. 'Neither are you, it would seem.'

'Nor you,' Andrew countered.

At that Jebb repacked his pipe and looked very smug. 'That's where you're wrong, matey, but it's a long story and I'm not going to tell it.'

'Quits,' said Andrew. 'And I'm not telling mine.'

Jebb roared with laughter. 'Close couple of buggers.'

Doctor Martin Goodfellow himself came to see Andrew in a state of great excitement at the prospect of going to England. 'You've saved my bacon, sir.'

That 'sir' shook Andrew. *Do I look that old?* 'Andrew's the name.' He settled that.

'Reckon I can't thank you enough – er – Andrew. I knew I couldn't leave the old codger to manage on his own. Has a bit of trouble with anno domini. Getting past it. You'll have worked that out for yourself. Keeps a jar of leeches handy! Would you believe it?'

'They have their uses,' Andrew said mildly. 'Not often but occasionally.'

Somewhat abashed, Goodfellow nervously adjusted his spectacles. 'Anyhow, it's sure good of you to take on the old man. I reckon he'll have to raise your salary. You're that much more experienced than I am.'

Andrew, on the contrary, was feeling very unsure of himself. He had not kept up with some of the latest medical thinking. Goodfellow's grasp of up-to-date drugs was impressive. 'The difficulty is,' he interrupted the other's flow, 'apart from a few weeks recently as ship's doctor, I have been practising since the war in an English country town. No sort of preparation for Australia's poisonous insects and snakes.'

'Don't worry,' Goodfellow tossed back his head as if he had no more use for it and gave Andrew the benefit of a full set of big, perfect teeth. Andrew had an insane urge to toss in a biscuit. Hole in one. But he sobered up immediately. Serious stuff this and he'd better listen.

'You Poms! Always the great drama about snakes and spiders and the like. We don't lose more than three or four a year.'

'Three or four what? Snakes or spiders?'

Goodfellow roared. 'People, man, people! Bloody care-less people. People not using their brains when they're out in the bush! You gotta make a noise and snakes'll get out of your way. Can't do much about it anyhow if you do get bitten except keep calm and say a requiem.' The giggle was disturbingly fifth-form. 'Honest, Andrew, after your job in the war, I would say there's nothing here you can't handle. I'll leave you my reference books. She'll be right.'

It seemed that Andrew's promotion to bush doctor was already settled. Only the date when he would take up his new appointment remained to be fixed. 'When are you leaving?'

'When you're ready to take over.'

'Christmas?' Andrew suggested.

'Great! Snowballs and Christmas pudding.'

'The cold will kill you, 'Andrew added pleasantly. 'Take some woolly long-johns.'

Norah thought it an excellent idea. Marian pouted, 'But we won't see so much of you.'

In the early part of 1965, exactly three years since he sailed from Tilbury as ship's doctor on the *Nevis,* Andrew stepped into the post of Dr Jebb's assistant and moved into Goodfellow's house in Ironstone. Marian drove him and his possessions in the truck since Norah was occupied with dressings in the clinic.

'Don't forget about us in Dog Creek,' she pleaded. 'We've got used to having you around.'

'I'll be making the usual visit to the clinic,' he assured her. 'And I can still take Reg for a fortune at pontoon.'

It was a poky little house. He opened wide the windows to let the fresh air in and the smell of menthol throat lozenges out. He was quite pleased to be living alone again and felt sure that, although Norah would never admit it, she was probably just as relieved to have her house to herself again.

Fourteen

A ndrew had not realized just how much he had
been missing the practising of his profession and
he embraced his new appointment with enthusiasm. His
patients were vastly different from those in his country
practice in England and the challenge was stimulating.

At first, Marian helped by riding with him to locate distant
homesteads until he was familiar with the area and then it
was his purest pleasure to ride alone through the bush, rapt
in vast silences broken only by bird calls. A far cry, this,
from his deskbound practice in Ambleside.

The folk who lived in the bush were a stoical lot, sending for medical assistance only when they had exhausted
their own very comprehensive first aid. Indications of his
coming would be noticed while he was some distance
away and by the time he clattered up the dirt road to the
homestead, the tea would be brewed and a slice of home-
made cake would await him. In inclement weather there
would be something a little stronger than tea to restore
him. He was accepted as part of the local population and
content to be so.

For the first time in many years, he allowed himself a
modicum of self-esteem. This was his chosen profession
and he was back in the driving seat. There was nothing to
cause him any concern in the normal run of accidents and
ailments which he had to deal with and Dr Goodfellow's
library was rarely referred to.

More and more, Graham Jebb delegated to him the bulk of the work while he spent his time in a dilapidated chair with a bottle at hand and a book lying open on his convenient paunch, but he did pull himself together when Andrew insisted on time off.

These breaks of two or three days at a time he usually spent in Sydney's bohemian quarter at King's Cross. With its immigrant population from all over Europe it provided a lively contrast to Dog Creek. These 'New Australians' brought with them their own culture and transformed King's Cross into a place of artists, musicians, dancers and wild exotic women. Andrew never discussed with Norah what he got up to on these visits and she never enquired. What was certain was that he always came back to Dog Creek with a monumental hangover.

At least once a week the Russells and the Reeds gathered at Norah's house for cards and gossip and a glass or two. Once or twice Andrew allowed himself to wonder how would it be if he stayed on even after Goodfellow's return. The life suited him down to the ground and the old doc could not go on for ever. He was well over seventy years old now, 'and shaky', Norah confirmed.

Fate seemed to nudge him in this direction when a request came from Goodfellow in England to extend his time in England for a further year so that he night undertake a course in plastic surgery. Andrew agreed to this extra year without reservation.

At the end of a busy morning clinic Norah brought him coffee. 'All your patients seem to be getting better.'

'That's the way I like it.' He took the cup from her and sank into one of her newly purchased comfortable chairs. Thanks to Daddy Watts's imaginative conversion of the old clinic, Norah now had a much larger sitting room and a good kitchen with an electric stove.

'The new clinic makes such a difference,' Andrew said. 'I can see what I'm doing now.'

'Martin Goodfellow will be surprised. When is he expected back?'

'About six months. He's coming by air to save time.'

'Not money. Will you stay on? We're all hoping you will.'

'Manners to wait until you're invited.'

Norah laughed. 'Graham will go down on bended knees.' She stirred her coffee vigorously. 'I'd miss you, Andrew, if you were to go home.'

He blew her a kiss. 'That's the nearest you have ever got to a declaration of love.'

'Don't let it go to your head. You know me.'

'I think I do.' he returned in the same light vein.

'More coffee?'

Andrew held out his cup. 'I'd like to see more of Simon and Cathy and Ray, yet if I were to leave here I know I would miss you all. After all, Saint Norah, you dragged me from the jaws of death.' He gave her a wide smile.

'And the Russells and Marian and Reg, the boys at the garage and Top Hat. All my friends. Incidentally, we haven't seen much of Reg lately. Is he all right?'

'Marian is cross with him. He's drinking too much. Goes to the Diggers' with his boozy mates instead of cards with us.'

A slight frown crossed Andrew's face. 'He's carrying far too much weight. I'll have a word with him. Could have high blood pressure.'

'He flew off the handle when I suggested a diet.'

The opportunity to speak confidentially to Reg did not arise for some time. Andrew approached Marian. 'I think Reg should come in for a check-up.'

'I know. He's too fat.'

'Could you book him in?'

'I'll get a rude answer but there's no harm in trying. He never used to be like this. Always a big hunk of a bloke but not obese and that is what he is now.'

'On second thoughts,' said Andrew, 'leave it. I'll choose my moment.' It was going to be tricky anyway and better that Marian was not involved.

The opportunity arrived on the day of Dog Creek Swimming Gala: flags and balloons, beer stalls, barbecued steak and sausages and a free-for-all boxing event with a crate of Fosters lager for the winner. The riverside was decked for carnival. Three of Top Hat's skinny little children were taking part in a race so Norah and Marian were pledged to attend. One of the Wilcox boys was starting a book and the bets were coming fast and furious.

'Reg should have come,' Norah complained. 'He would have enjoyed this.'

'He's got a fit of the blues. Do men have a change of life, Norah? Because I think that's what he's having.'

Reg had waited until the women set off for the river then he sought out Andrew. He was in the treatment room at the clinic preparing ointment.

Andrew looked up in pleased surprise. 'Reg. Just the bloke I want to see.'

Without any greeting, Reg flung himself down heavily into a chair and buried his head in his hands. He did not speak.

Disturbed by his silence, Andrew approached him. 'Are you all right?'

Reg shook his bullish head and mumbled something so indistinctly that Andrew was not sure if he had heard aright. 'What did you say?' He spoke quite sharply.

Reg lifted his head and looked straight at Andrew displaying an expression of such malevolence that Andrew drew back in surprise.

'What I said was, there's not a bloody soul here in Dog

Creek or anywhere else for that matter who cares a piss about me.'

'What on earth are you on about, Reg? You have friends everywhere you go.'

'If your wife no longer loves you, friends count for nothing.'

Andrew frowned in confusion, embarrassed by this very personal disclosure. 'Surely you're mistaken, old chap.'

'Don't you "old chap" me.' Reg sprang to his feet, thrusting his face to within a few inches of Andrew's. His customary good humour was distorted by hate. His eyes glittered, black and threatening. 'You should know better than anyone, you bastard!' He was shouting, his face contused with anger.

Andrew pulled back from the flying spittle. *My God*, he thought, *he's working himself up to a heart attack.* 'I don't get your drift,' he said calmly in an attempt to take the heat out of the confrontation.

'My "drift", as you put it,' Reg spat, 'is that my wife is in love with you and don't you damn well know it!'

The accusation hit Andrew like a thunderbolt. So outrageous was the suggestion that he was temporarily lost for words. Then the high tide of anger swamped him. 'Now look here—'

'No, Doc, y*ou look here*! Ever since you came she's been making sheep's eyes at you. No time for me. And I've seen how you egged her on with your sly jokes and suggestive remarks. And when her mother was laid up recently it was you she came to for comfort, not me!'

'Because I'm a doctor, you nut!'

Reg brushed this aside. 'It was, "Andrew says this" and "Andrew says that" till I got sick to death of the sound of your name. That's what's making me ill. That's why I'm drinking too much, why my heart is bangin' away fit to bust. And I warn you that if you don't get

121

out of town quick sharp I'll knock your bloody Pommie block off.'

Andrew made an effort to control his anger. 'I am more sorry than I can say that you should think this of me. It is entirely a figment of your imagination. I have no thoughts of you or Marian except as my very good friends. At least that is how it has been until this moment. I can assure you, Reg, that I have never had any designs on your wife's affections.'

Reg banged the table with his dangerous fist. 'Jesus! You don't expect me to swallow that garbage.'

Andrew persisted. 'And I am quite sure she feels the same way about me, simply a friend. But I am leaving soon.' He was suddenly making decisions. 'My contract expires when Goodfellow returns in six weeks time. I sincerely hope that you will realize how mistaken you are and that we may part friends.'

'Get stuffed.' Reg reached for his cattleman's hat. 'And get going!' The door crashed behind him making the medicine bottles rattle on the shelves. Even after he had gone, the treatment room seemed to shiver with the violence of his visit.

Andrew sank on to a stool, his thoughts in a turmoil. Not having been prepared in any way for this unprovoked and unjustified attack he could only dimly comprehend the imminent upheaval in his life caused by this quarrel with Reg. His own anger was settling into something cold and heavy within him. This was an emotion he recognized. He had been here before, on the beach at Dunkirk and again when Hilde turned him down. All his recently regained lightness of spirit was rapidly draining away as though his very being was a sieve and once again he would be left with the dregs.

Apart from his own feelings of injustice, Andrew was genuinely worried over Reg's state of health. He desperately wanted to confide in Norah but decided against it. The knowledge of what had passed between himself and Reg would undoubtedly produce a rift in her future relations with the Russells, especially with Marian, her closest friend.

He must take himself off. He had no choice. Where, he did not know. Australia was a huge continent. He would clear out and leave the place which had welcomed him when he came as a stranger almost ten years ago to live amongst them. Dog Creek for him had been a sanctuary, a refuge from the 'slings and arrows of outrageous fortune' with which he was very familiar. He could tell Shakespeare a thing or two about outrageous fortune. Story of his life.

The sense of injustice weighed heavily upon him. It was all so unfair. A warm friendship existed between himself and the two women, nothing more. Marian had never made the slightest move towards a more intimate relationship. Had she done so, Andrew himself would have nipped it in the bud. He had no leanings towards other men's wives and Marian wanted no one but her own man, who was very dear to her.

The sound of the women's voices approaching the clinic broke into the disarray of his thoughts. Norah and Marian were returning from the gala. He jumped to his feet and took up the mortar and pestle he had been using. He snatched his mind away from the word-for-word repeats of the scene with Reg and found a smile to welcome the women.

'I won this for you.' Marian thrust a coconut into his arms. 'Knocked all the skittles down in one throw.'

'And I scored a bullseye at the rifle range and brought you this.' Norah handed him a china butter dish with a naked lady lounging on the lid. The two women collapsed in laughter and Andrew did his best to join their lighthearted mood.

'What's up with Reg?' Marian was still smiling though her eyes keenly searched Andrew's face. 'We met him as we came in. Looked like his face had slipped. Not my usual Sunny Jim.'

'He's not keen on my idea that he should try to lose weight.'

Marian accepted that. 'It's the beer. I wish they'd close the damn Diggers' down.'

All Andrew wanted at that moment was to be left alone with his problem. He cleared away his work and excused himself, leaving the two women to their tea.

As he drove back to Ironstone his mind went over every detail in that extraordinary encounter with Reg. He realized that nothing would convince Reg that he was making a mistake. He dreaded facing Norah with the fact that he was leaving but leave he must before more trouble was caused within the Russell family.

Dr Jebb, too, must be informed. There would be questions on all sides. All thoughts of staying on and eventually taking over the practice when Jebb retired had flown. He must prepare to leave when Goodfellow returned. He had six weeks in which to make his arrangements.

Graham Jebb was surprised and disappointed to learn that Andrew meant to move on. 'Well, now,' he rubbed his two-day stubble in perplexity. 'I was thinking you were going to put your swag down here for good?'

His voice coaxed an explanation but Andrew did not respond.

'Something good turned up?' Jebb persisted. He was more upset than he showed. He'd taken a great liking to this younger man. A lonely old age stared him in the face. No medical chats, no one to listen to his memories of the Fitzroy Tavern.

Andrew saw the self-pity welling up in the crumpled face and was desperately sorry to do this to the old chap who had never been other than friendly towards him. 'I'll stay till Goodfellow is back in harness and then I must move on.'

But he gave no reason and Jebb spent many days after Andrew had gone puzzling over this sudden departure but never touched on the absurd truth.

Andrew was ill at ease when he next encountered Marian. He watched carefully for any sign that might justify Reg's suspicions but he could detect no personal overtures in her behaviour. She was the same happy-go-lucky friendly creature as always, a cool kiss on the cheek such as she might have given to a favourite uncle, joking, laughing and gossiping as always.

'What's the matter with you today, Sobersides?' she chaffed him for his solemn mood. 'Get out of bed the wrong side did you?'

Andrew looked up and saw that Reg was watching him like a cat with a mouse.

'A lot of things on my mind.' He pointedly did not look at Marian. 'Like how do I convince a patient of mine that he is wrong about his condition when he is convinced he is right.'

Norah, pouring drinks, considered this. 'If you are right, time will prove it.'

Andrew had no plans, no idea where to go. Despairingly he took stock of his lodgings which Goodfellow would soon reclaim. His personal weighty medical literature filled the shelves, his precious case of instruments, bought on a wave of exultation when he gained his medical degree, his collection of long-playing records and a host of small useless things which he could not throw away, all these must be packed and transported. Where? Destination unknown. People said Adelaide was a fine city. Or Perth, good climate. Or Sydney? Set up a practice in King's Cross for druggies and wine-ohs and become one himself? Not likely.

First, he must break the news to Norah that he was leaving and, since he knew she would smell a rat, he began concocting a believable lie to explain his decision.

He sat up late that night smoking too many cigarettes and thinking. That phrase Reg used – 'My "drift" as you put it, is that my wife is in love with you and don't you damn well know it' – kept running through his head. He was unrefreshed when he drove to Dog Creek the next morning to break the news to Norah that he was leaving.

Fifteen

The wet season had begun. In Goodfellow's old Holden Andrew drove through clouds of vapour as torrential rain hit the hot, baked earth. Sections of the road from Ironstone to Dog Creek were already under six inches of water and collapsing at the edges but he pressed on. He must see Norah without delay.

He was still turning over in his mind plausible reasons for his hasty exit from the company of so many friends in order to go – where? He had no idea where. He had no plans, only bitterness at the unfairness of life. Bitterness, hurt and helplessness. Hell. Why did Reg have to spoil it all?

The tin roof of the carport at the clinic clattered under the deluge and roof gutters, running full, cascaded their contents into the 500-gallon tank adjoining the building, safeguarding the clinic's water supply against the droughts which would surely follow. He parked the Holden and, still without a definite plan of action, went in search of Norah.

He found her standing, deep in thought, by the mail box under a dripping lemon tree, with a letter in her hand. The rain, unheeded, plastered her hair to her head and deepened the puddle she was standing in. For the moment, Andrew forgot his errand. His shout pulled her back to reality.

'Norah! What on earth are you doing, standing out there in the rain? You look like a drowned rat.'

She looked up. 'A letter from Cathy. Ray has died. Pneumonia.'

'A-ah! I'm sorry.' He took her arm and hustled her inside, handed her a dry towel for her hair.

'Following flu.'

'He hadn't much of a chance with only one good lung.' Andrew took the towel from her since she was making no move to dry herself and tousled her hair for her. 'Poor chap. He wasn't very old.'

'According to Cathy, he was coming up to his sixtieth birthday. She will be utterly devastated. He was the love of her life.'

'I'll make some coffee.' Andrew's problem had temporarily receded in the face of Norah's distress. It could wait. He put water to boil and fetched two mugs.

When he came back with the coffee, he found Norah quite composed. 'I must go home now, Andrew.' She tucked the letter back into its damp envelope.

'Home?' he queried.

'England. Cathy will need me. Forgive me for deserting you.' She kicked off her soggy sandals and took the steaming cup from Andrew.

It took only a minute for Andrew to grasp the fact that here was a solution to his problem. 'My contract here finishes next month,' he heard himself saying calmly. 'I will come with you.'

Marian found the situation completely incomprehensible. 'What about the clinic?'

'I've found a well qualified nurse from Sydney who wants to work in the country. The Health Authority has vetted her. She's OK.'

'What does poor old Jebb think about all this, not only your departure but Andrew's as well?'

'Goodfellow will be back next week.'

Seated at her desk, making a list of instructions for the new nurse, Norah became aware of Marian standing over

127

her in hostile silence, arms folded, feet apart, belligerence expressed in every line of her stance.

'I'm sorry to cause all this disturbance,' Norah explained. 'But I must go to Cathy, my old friend, when she needs me.'

'And what about me?' Marian was not joking. Her voice was cold. 'What about our friendship? Does that count for nothing?

Norah hung her head. 'Don't make it difficult for me, Marian. You know there will always be a close relationship between us. You and Reg must come and visit me in England.'

'Some chance of that!' Marian snorted. Angrily she turned to look out of the streaming window. 'And after all,' she confronted Norah, 'it was my brother you were supposed to be marrying at one time.'

Norah looked up quickly.

Marian sighed. 'You never fooled me, Norah. At first, perhaps. Later I realized that you were an under-sexed filly. You are just not cut out for a physical relationship with a man. Nor with a woman, for that matter. Look at your one doomed venture into marriage. OK. I accepted that. The only thing that mattered to me was that Keith loved you and had asked you to marry him. You gave him happiness before he died. For that, I love you, Norah. The fact that you turned him down is neither here nor there and did not come between us in any way. But now you are leaving and I will miss you more than I can say.'

Norah got up from her seat and hugged her close. 'I was truly fond of your brother, Marian. You must believe me. To offer more than that was beyond me. Don't ask me why. I don't know. But he never knew that I had rejected him. My letter was returned unopened.' She sank back into her chair, hiding her face in her hands.

Softening at Norah's distress, Marian said gently. 'It

doesn't matter. I suppose I will get used to your absence, eventually. It has been such fun, our rides through the bush, swimming in the waterhole, gin and gossip as the sun went down.'

'I will never forget Wirrawee and you.' Begging a reconciliation, Norah lifted brimming eyes.

'And perhaps Reg and I will hop on a plane one day and come knocking at your door.'

'Tell me one thing, Marian. Does your mother share your beliefs about Keith and myself?'

'Oh no. And she never will.'

'I'm glad about that.'

'You have been a comfort to my father and mother and a great mate to me whether or not you were meant to be part of the family.' She bent to drop a light kiss on Norah's forehead. 'So when you go, you go with our love and the hopes that we might meet again. One thing puzzles me.' She had begun her customary pacing about, whacking her boot with her crop to aid the thinking process. 'Why did you accept our invitation in the first place, knowing that you never would have married Keith?'

Norah coloured with guilt. 'That was unforgiveable of me, but I eased my conscience by telling myself that Keith had always said he wanted to bring me here, to Australia, to Wirrawee and, more than that, wanted me to come, even if he were killed, to visit his family and his country, to understand what he was fighting for. I persuaded myself that I was only doing what he would have liked me to do. Added to that, I was desperately unhappy in England.'

'Because of Cathy's marriage to someone with a history of TB?'

'To someone who could never be the equal of Simon.' She checked herself. 'Of course I am sorry that Ray has died, but given his early history, it is surprising that he lived to be sixty.'

Marian nodded but whether in acquiescence with Norah's mood or confirmation of her own opinion was hard to tell. She made to go. 'I must see to the horses,' and turned at the door. 'Can't you stay for Christmas? I'm riding at Buller's Flat. And, another thing, why must Andrew go too? To lose both of you is hard tack for Reg and me to stomach.'

'I know nothing of Andrew's business.'

Left alone, Norah turned her attention to labelling her luggage. Number 21. The Green. Epping. Essex, she wrote. C/o Mrs R.Webster. Epping would seem as tight as a shoe box after Australia's wide-open spaces but go she must, although it had to be admitted that Cathy had made no such suggestion.

Saying goodbye to Mary and Dan was the hardest part. They were both in their eighties now. Mary was greatly incapacitated by arthritis and Dan had handed over the greater part of the management to Reg who had a hired man to help with the heavy work.

Mary cried a little, seeing the last thread with her son's wartime experiences broken but she was nevertheless bravely understanding. 'Of course you must go back to your own country, my dear. You leave many happy memories of your time spent with us.'

Norah took her leave of a gloomy Doctor Jebb. 'The nurse taking my place knows her job,' she consoled him, 'and Rose is a reliable assistant.'

She held an auction sale of her goods at the Diggers' Hotel and persuaded Reg to oversee the letting of her house or the sale of it if a suitable buyer turned up.

Then there was one more important business to attend to. Some weeks previously, on a trip to Sydney with Marian, she had noted a splendid opera top hat in a second-hand shop on the Military Road in Neutral Bay with the thought that, at a suitable time, she would present it to her aboriginal friend who had been a loyal helper to her ever since the first days of her coming to Dog Creek.

Now was the right time. Top Hat was overjoyed. His huge smile of gleaming teeth conveyed his pride as he posed for a photograph wearing his prize that was also his title.

She was reassured by the warmth of Reg's farewell. He had been strangely distant of late, foregoing visits to her house in favour of the company of sharp characters at the Diggers', but his hug at their parting confirmed that all was well between them. 'You're a dinkum sheila all right, Norah, and we're all going to miss you a lot.'

She was packed and ready to go, ready to leave the little house which had grown from a humpy to a respectable – if unorthodox – home thanks to Daddy Watts. It had been his last, and most adventurous, undertaking before they carried him up the hill to the graveyard under the sweet-smelling pittosporum trees.

She sat at her desk for the last time and wrote a quick note to Cathy.

> I'm on my way. Let me do the worrying. Probably
> arrive Christmas morning with Santa Claus.
> My love, as always,
> Norah.
> PS Put a HWB in my bed. I know I shall freeze.

Reg flew her and Andrew in the Auster to Sydney airport. If Andrew had hoped for a last-minute return to reason on Reg's part he was disappointed. He sat behind that unforgiving neck and stubborn shoulders all the way from Ironstone to Mascot and when Reg took his leave of them to return to Dog Creek not a glance, not a word was directed his way.

This odd behaviour did not escape Norah's notice. It seemed odd, but Reg was no doubt anxious to get back to Wirrawee as soon as possible.

'See you in the UK.' Andrew shepherded Norah to her departure lounge. He himself hoped to take the leisurely way home by sea. 'You'll be home long before me.'

He intended to visit the shipping quarter of Sydney as soon as Norah was airborne and hoped to work his passage once more as a ship's doctor. The long sea trip to England, away from the trauma of the last few weeks in Australia, was what he yearned for. There, among strangers, he would find renewed peace of mind.

The concourse at Sydney airport was dressed overall for Christmas with tinsel and glitter. Andrew's was the only glum face in the hustling, bustling crowds.

From the plane window Norah looked out on her last view of the sunburnt country – the blue, blue sky and the girls in pretty summer dresses, the baking, benevolent sun – and she reminded herself that when she descended at Heathrow, London, the day would be cold. There might even be snow. There would be blue noses and fur-lined boots and chilblains but there would also be Cathy. She was happy to be on her way home, but her thoughts were tinged with sadness. Australia had been kind to her. Andrew's decision to return to the UK had surprised her. He had seemed to enjoy life in Australia and particularly his country practice. But that was his affair. They would meet up again in Britain.

Sixteen

It was Christmas Eve in Sydney; 100 degrees in the shade. Despite the heat the streets teemed like an ant heap. Andrew's frustration was rising with the temperature as short-tempered crowds, burdened with parcels, pushed and shoved in their struggle to complete the last-minute agenda for Christmas day. Flip-flopping sandals beat a path from store to store where the saga of Good King Wenceslas at full volume fought for precedence over the fanfare of cash registers. Steamy students in red gowns and white whiskers bounced sticky children on their knees and wished them all to hell.

With relief Andrew left the hysteria of the shopping centre and headed for the road leading down to the docks where shipping offices nudged each other for space. Here, the dearth of traffic, the funereal silence after the clamour of the shops was the first indication of a miscalculation in his plans, quickly confirmed when one shipping office after another presented closed doors and the message 'CLOSED FOR THE CHRISTMAS HOLIDAYS'.

Andrew's hopes faded away. He had not taken into account such immovables as early closing and office parties. He should have booked a hotel. Fat chance of finding any with vacancies now, on Christmas Eve, in a city hell-bent on having a good time.

His suitcases were pulling his arms out. Sweat poured off him. His shirt stuck to his back and it was all Reg's fault.

Reg had put him in this ridiculous situation. With murder in his heart he walked to the last but one of the shipping offices where a miracle was waiting to happen.

The entrance door was not exactly open but neither was it exactly shut and what raised his hopes more than anything else was the name on the brass plate – 'The Blue Sea Line', the line which had employed him on his outward voyage, the line Ray had worked for. Ray had been a good friend to him. He was sad to think he would not see him again.

He pushed open the door, parked his suitcases in the passage, paused and listened. There was silence; no sound of business, no ring of a typewriter, not a single footfall nor whine of a lift until the unmistakable groan of a vacuum cleaner started up. Andrew was up the stairs in a moment seeking the operator and came face to face with a handsome youth in a tee shirt and brief shorts engaged in sucking up dirt with a snaking hose. 'We're closed, mate,' he greeted Andrew cheerfully above the din. 'Find yourself a party to go to.' When his visitor continued to mouth questions, he obligingly shut off the motor. 'One of the secretaries is still here,' he thumbed the next floor up. 'But she will not be happy to see you. She's ropeable.'

Andrew was already halfway up the next flight of stairs. The sound of a woman's voice led him to a large office which showed every sign of a recent celebration. Sagging paper decorations and withering balloons, empty crisp packets, discarded Coca Cola cans overflowing the waste paper bins and, alone amid the post-party detritus, a young woman, seemingly the sole representative of the Blue Sea Shipping Company still working, was speaking on the phone. All the desks around her were tidied up for the holidays, typewriters under cover. Her own desk was littered with official-looking documents. To judge from her harassed appearance, this was not a good moment to intervene. Andrew hesitated at the open door. 'Excuse me.'

She looked up in dismay. 'We're closed,' she said, not unkindly but brusquely. 'Come back on January 3rd.'

The cleaner had been right. She was definitely not pleased to see him. She was young and pretty but buttoned-up with worry. Andrew's hope of booking a passage today drained away. She had enough problems of her own without listening to his.

'I'm sorry,' she said, relenting a little, 'but we're closed for the Christmas holidays. There's an emergency on right now. That's why I'm here. To deal with it. This lot,' angrily she pointed to the abandoned desks, 'have scarpered.'

'Sorry to be a nuisance,' Andrew apologized. 'I'll get out of your hair right now. I was hoping I might pick up a passage to the UK as ship's doctor. I came out on one of your ships in that capacity a few years ago and I was hoping there might be a chance today, but I'll deal with that later. You have your own problems.' With a sincere 'Happy Christmas' he turned to go.

Her screech electrified him. 'You're a doctor? And you want to go to Britain? Oh Glory! Glory! My guardian angel is back on duty. Take a seat, sir.' She pulled up a chair for him. 'I'll get you a Scotch or something. PLEASE don't go away.'

Baffled at her change of mood, Andrew somewhat tentatively took the seat she offered and watched as she rooted about in her desk, found a clean paper cup and drained a bottle of Scotch for him.

'We've got a sick sailor on our hands,' she explained. 'He's in Sydney Hospital at the moment and they want him out, like, now. We've got to fly him to Scotland with a medical escort but there's not a doctor in Sydney prepared to up sticks and fly to Aberdeen on Christmas Eve.'

Haltingly, preparing herself for another polite refusal, she asked, 'I don't suppose you would take on the job?'

No, thought Andrew, I certainly don't want to go as medical escort by plane to the UK. I am looking forward to a nice, long, lazy trip by sea among people who do not know me from Adam. A breathing space is what I want. So why did he hesitate? It was madness but the poor girl was clearly desperate. And it was Christmas Eve, after all.

'You would be well paid, I'm telling you.'

Andrew frowned. That had nothing to do with the proposition. 'Hold on.' She had gone wild with excitement at first and now tears were threatening. Everything was happening too quickly. Common sense was slipping away. 'I'm hoping to go by sea,' he protested, but his brain was working overtime and his conscience was all squared up for a debate.

'The company will certainly make it worth your while. I can vouch for that.' She was ready to promise him the moon so that she could shut up shop and join the other girls at Toni's Fish Place on the harbour, but she could detect no message of hope in this English doctor blown in from nowhere. 'The bosses are already making for their beach houses.' A note of desperation and disappointment crept into her voice. 'It's all right for them. I've been invited to a party tonight and I haven't washed my hair yet. Haven't even ironed my dress.'

Andrew saw and glanced away from the suspicious glistening in her eyes. 'What's the matter with this sailor?'

Resignedly and with frankness she recounted his damning diagnosis. 'Delirium tremens. Pink elephants and snakes. He went berserk with a sledgehammer on the voyage out and the crew refuses to sail with him again. They've already left without him and the hospital is going to ditch him with me at any minute. Christmas Eve with a metho for company! How's that for a wild scenario?' She sniffed hugely. 'It's bloody well not fair.' She fumbled for a tissue. 'I've rung up every GP in Sydney, but who in their right mind would give up the BBQ with the kids and the parties, to fly to Aberdeen in the middle of winter? Aberdeen!' she squealed. 'I ask you!'

136

Andrew did a quick review. He could not help but admire her gutsy honesty and made up his mind to do the decent thing, although what on earth he would do in Aberdeen on Christmas Eve was beyond his imagination. But this young lady, who was dabbing her eyes and pouring residual gin dregs into her coffee cup, would be able to go to her party after all, iron her frock and wash her hair.

'I'll do it,' he said, welcoming the warm feeling of chivalry, fleeting though it was. 'You shall go to the ball, Cinderella.' It was so long since he had smiled that his face seemed to crack with the effort.

She jumped up and it seemed for a moment that she was about to hug him till she thought better of it. 'You saint! You cracker bonza bloke!' She was laughing and crying all at once. 'I must phone my boss. He'll be ecstatic. Yes, Mr Grainger,' she exploded into the phone. 'Just walked in off the street. Yes, English. Sailed with us before as ship's doctor.'

Andrew heard a gasp on the other end of the phone and a male voice asking, 'Is his name Christopher by any chance?'

Bob Grainger's entrance was nothing if not dramatic. Youngish, baldish and portly, his face wreathed in smiles, he was heralded by a jubilation of car keys and the percussion of doors. He began extending his handshake to Andrew as he came through the door. He wore a tight, white tee shirt inscribed 'I Do It Rare'. His shorts were very short and his thighs were massive. Andrew was beginning to think he should go away and come back several days later but his hand was firmly held.

'Come into my office,' said the jolly director and, to his secretary, 'Stick around, Kerry. Let's get this thing sewn up.' He pointed Andrew to a chair and produced a bottle of Scotch and two glasses. 'Scuse the rig,' he scratched his

137

crotch. 'I'm in the middle of a family barbecue. Now, Dr Mount, how d'ye like your whisky?'

'I'll take it neat,' said Andrew. 'Looks like I'm going to need it.'

So here he was in a curtained-off section of a plane bound for the north of Scotland in charge of a deeply sedated, raving mad sailor from Stornoway.

There was plenty of time during the long flight to review his situation, to relive his time in Australia and recall the friends he had made and would never see again. He remembered with pride his odd little practice in the bush and his stoical patients, worthy descendants of fearless pioneers. When he thought of Norah – she would be half way to Singapore by now – he remembered how she had nursed him back to health after peritonitis. He owed her a great deal and hoped to meet up with her once more when his life – and hers – had settled. Not for the first time, Andrew wondered if Norah was doing the right thing by dropping everything she held dear in Australia to go and live with Cathy. Andrew had never shared Norah's coolness towards Ray, in his opinion a first-class chap, and his marriage with Cathy which had so concerned Norah was surely ordained, so complete was their devotion to each other. To rush to Cathy's side so soon after Ray's death might not be the panacea she thought it was. She must surely realize that she could not turn the clock back.

His patient stirred and muttered a stream of obscenities. Time for another injection. He looked at the man who was killing himself with alcohol. What was his future? Come to that, what was his own future? What awaited him in Aberdeen? In Scotland in midwinter?

He was offered lentil soup and haggis on the flight and he liked neither. Couldn't even drown his sorrows in whisky because he had a crazy patient to look after. He allowed himself a cat nap while his patient reverted to stentorian snoring and

138

when he opened his eyes the plane had begun its descent, through the mists to a land covered with snow.

Once his patient had been transferred by waiting ambulance to the Aberdeen Neurological Centre, the airport staff melted away on the trail of roast goose and Christmas pudding and Andrew's responsibilities were at an end. Shivering in the intense cold, he scanned the deserted streets of the granite city for a taxi. Winds with snow on their breath sliced through every bit of his clothing. He had intended to stock up on winter clothes from the excellent store of such items on board ship. His unplanned trip by air left him with only a summer-weight Australian suit between him and the northern winter. He had a wallet full of money and no overcoat and he prayed for a taxi before he died of hypothermia.

His prayer was answered in the form of an idling taxi with a driver who had nobody at home to cook a dinner for him. He was rugged up to the chin in a thick padded jacket. Andrew jumped aboard with the speed of a gazelle.

'Get me to a shop where I can buy a jacket like yours,' he ordered. 'Quick!'

His instructions were treated with a sardonic laugh. 'Ye'll nae doot ken it's Christmas Day.'

Andrew had forgotten, of course – again.

'And there's nae shop of any sort whatever ye'll find open today.' The driver squinted in the cab mirror. 'Ye're no properly dressed for this part of the world. Where ha' ye come frae?'

Andrew had no time for jokey taxi drivers. 'Australia,' he barked, 'and I'm about to catch pneumonia. I want a warm jacket like yours and I want somewhere to stay, right now.'

'I'll tak ye to a decent place wi' good food and clean beds and I'll sell ye ma jacket for twenty pund.'

'Done. Hand it over and step on the gas.'

Seventeen

N orah's return to England came as a surprise to Cathy, especially her decision not to return to Australia.

'Of course not, Cat. Not when you need me here.'

Cathy was a little ill at ease. Their years apart, despite regular correspondence, required time for readjustment. Cathy's own grief, which was overwhelming, was a calamity outside of Norah's experience. A small voice within her cried out that she needed to be left alone with her children for a while, to adjust to the empty seat at the table, the empty place in her bed, the huge hole in her life, the loss of her beloved.

The boys were brave for her sake and trod lightly through fragile conversations in fear of bringing fresh pain to their mother, and they welcomed the arrival of Aunt Norah from Australia as company for her. Not so with Alison. Alison was fourteen, the only one of Cathy's three children still at school. Philip was at university and Michael was a trainee in a metal refining company. Alison resented the intrusion into their family of this aunt from Australia, interfering at a time when they all specially needed to be alone.

Her father's death was a deeply-felt personal loss to Alison. He had been for her an icon of manhood. The man she would marry would have to measure up to her beloved Daddy, and now he was gone, snatched away before she'd had time to grow up. She saved her tears for private places and cried herself to sleep every night under the bedclothes. She did not want Aunt Norah to catch her with the flag down.

'Poor little Alison,' Norah would say and Alison cringed from her bony cuddle.

'You must rest,' Norah told Cathy. 'You've been under a lot of strain. First your father died and now Raymond.'

But rest was the last thing Cathy needed. 'If I have nothing to do,' she said, 'I will spend each day feeling sorry for myself.' She knew that her inner spring was overwound and, like the old clock in the dining room, she must tick along at her own pace until the imbalance righted itself – if it ever would. She worked through each day as it came and saw to the needs of her children. She had lost a husband but they had lost a father.

Philip and Michael were strong. They talked of Dad and remembered the things he used to say that always made them laugh, but there was no laughing now in the square stone house on the Green. There was crying. No one was game to sit in his favourite chair. It stood there by the fireside, waiting, arms outstretched, infinitely pathetic. His dictionary and pen were on the small table close by, waiting for the *Daily Telegraph* crossword. Waiting. The entire house was waiting, unaware that the master would not be returning. Into this mourning household came Norah, full of helpful suggestions and good deeds.

Simon came to call, to see if he could help Cathy to sort out Ray's affairs, and was astonished to find Norah in the kitchen. She was not quite the Norah he remembered before she went to live in Australia but then, he told himself, he had changed a fair bit too. Whereas Norah had become very skinny and stooped a little, he admitted he had put on weight.

'Great to see you old girl.' She presented a cool cheek and he obliged. 'Good of you to come.'

'I had to come home when Cathy needed me.'

141

'How long are you here for?'

'Oh, I'm not going back.'

That did surprise him. Oh well. None of his business. 'What's Andrew up to? Last I heard from him he was looking for a voyage home.'

'He should have arrived by now but we've had no news.'

'It was a bit sudden, wasn't it? His decision to come back to the UK?'

'It was a surprise to me too. He seemed to be happy in Australia. Lots of friends and he ran a great little clinic. I don't know why he suddenly decided to pack it all in.' Her mind flashed back for a second to that unexplained coolness between Andrew and Reg at Sydney airport. 'I don't know.'

He picked up his cap. 'Must be off. I'm based at Camberley now.'

'Cathy told me. Congratulations, Brigadier.'

'Thanks. I'm hanging on, doing inglorious work in admin. Not my cup of tea, but better than the scrap heap.' He took her by the hands, suddenly and intimately earnest. 'Call me, Norah, if she needs help. Call me and I'll come at once.'

Norah's self-imposed duty of helping Cathy did not get any easier as time went by. There seemed to be an unbridgeable gap between herself and Alison, although she made a conscious effort to be sympathetic towards the girl. Philip was away for most of the time. Michael was easy to get on with, a keen rugby player reminding Norah of Simon when he was young. In fact Simon frequently invited Michael to join him and his own two sons to watch an important match.

Norah met other difficulties apart from Alison's attitude. She began to see her role as superfluous. That hurt, but when she was honest, she had to face the fact that Cathy was self-sufficient and had no real need of her.

She had planned to give Cathy her breakfast in bed but Cathy was up first every day, bringing Norah a mug of tea. Norah would do the shopping but Cathy liked to choose the meat and vegetables herself. On the only occasion when Norah cooked the dinner it was a charred failure. 'Oh, I don't understand Agas,' she wailed and her confidence ebbed away.

In far-off Australia she had imagined that Cathy the widow would revert to Cathy the schoolfriend, that the years of their separation would be turned like the pages of a book and the story would continue to the bit that said, 'And they lived happily ever after.'

'I'm a fraud,' she confessed miserably. 'I came to help and I end up by being utterly useless.'

Cathy put an arm about her. 'Just the fact that you are here is a comfort, Norah darling. To be able to talk to you about Ray, about the old days and the fun we had together helps me to face a future without him.'

Norah accepted this.

'Help as much as you like, but do not try to make a patient out of me,' Cathy warned.

There was a better understanding between them after that. When Cathy announced that she was taking the dog for a walk, Norah saw that she wanted to go alone. Norah claimed certain household chores as her responsibility and earned Brownie points at last from Alison by insisting that the washing up was her job.

'The trouble is,' she admitted, 'at Dog Creek I made the rules. I believe I have become rather bossy.'

Cathy smiled. 'Poor Andrew.'

Norah glanced at the calendar on the wall. 'I wonder where he is now. Probably still at sea. He promised to get in touch as soon as he arrived.'

Andrew's accommodation, as recommended by the taxi

driver, was a draughty room in a draughty hotel which reeked of fried fish and boiled cabbage. He located a freezing cold bathroom at the end of a freezing cold passage. After a scant bath he sent down to the bar for a bottle of single malt before climbing into a freezing cold bed. He was extremely unhappy. Scots and their neeps and their tatties he cursed and their bloody fynnon haddie. But when the malt ambrosia trickled through his veins he forgave them all.

He put off writing to Norah until he had regulated his body clock which continued to operate on Australian time for some days, waking at 3 a.m. and dropping asleep at noon. He could not bear to think of Dog Creek. It was too painful. He missed the warm circle of friends he had known there. He missed the sunshine, he missed Marian's gentle mother, Mary, tearful to see him go. He missed the busy little clinic and Top Hat – and Norah, competent, kindly, Norah, whom the chaps back home used to call 'the ice maiden'. Maiden, maybe, but the ice had long since melted.

He was back on the lonely side of life. He would stir himself soon, he told himself, when he had readjusted to life in Britain. He would contact Simon. Simon was now a disgruntled brigadier retired to an administrative job in the grazing fields of Camberley. He would have the latest news of old friends, of Alec in Canada and Eric, the only one of the old bunch to be still living in Eastport. And he would write to Cathy, of course. Poor Cathy. Hers was such a fairy-tale romance that started in a most unlikely fashion in the sick bay of a hospital. Now she had lost her dear Raymond. He could picture her despair.

Soberly he returned to his own situation. He acknowledged that, sooner or later, he must look for a job. At fifty-four he was not yet ready to be put out to grass. Surgical registrar at the Aberdeen Royal Infirmary perhaps? His varied experience in Australia would stand him in good stead. Or he might take a refresher course in Ear, Nose and Throat. Or move on. Where to?

He did none of these things. As the last days of 1970 slipped away he became less and less inclined to make any move whatsoever, although it was a dismal hotel offering dismal food run by dreary, dismal people. He moped in his room and drank too much.

On New Year's Eve there were sounds of revelry in the street outside the hotel, bagpipes in the market place, fireworks in the park, but he did not bother to investigate. The next morning he went out in his taxi-driver jacket to buy a newspaper, to see how the rest of the world was faring without him, for he had no part in their affairs. He did not belong anywhere. He might just as well stay here, pickled in whisky, coddled and fattened on haggis and spotted dick puddings, a totally useless person.

'Ay've lit a fire in the lounge.' This New Year resolution of the proprietress was as yet untarnished. 'Ye'll maybe prefer to sit there awhile with your paper seeing as it's a wee bitty cold today.' As though they had been sunbathing up till now. But he thanked her cordially and acted upon her advice, appropriating for himself one of the two easy chairs by the fireside.

He spread his paper. 'Yesterday's, ye'll mind,' the newsagent had said with what Andrew interpreted as malicious pleasure. It was John Knox at his nefarious business again, no doubt. 'Ye shall not enjoy thyself on New Year's Day.' No matter. There was nothing to do anyhow. He would take a look down the Honours List to see if anyone he knew was mentioned – and was instantly electrified.

The name that jumped off the page was that of Hilde Mullerman, who had been made a Dame of the British Empire for her humanitarian services to refugees. Reading on, he learnt that she had opened not one but several homes in the north of England where the dispossessed and

homeless could find sanctuary and Sanctuary was the name
by which she wished these centres to be known. 'Mullerman
Sanctuaries.'

Just the sight of her name set a cold grip on his heart and
banished every other thought from his head. Was he never
to rid himself of his futile devotion to her? He was nothing
to her. Never had been. Yet from the first time he met her he
was lost. He closed his eyes to shut out the pain of the past,
those five long years of hoping only to be rejected. Her face
swam into focus, the serene oval face with its high cheek
bones and dark lustrous eyes. Andrew had seen those eyes
swimming with unshed tears and filled with love, but not for
him. For her patients, who meant everything in the world to
her, leaving no room for him. He had been foolish enough
to imagine that the affection she undoubtedly felt for him
would grow to love. Instead it fizzled to nothing, like hairs
on a hot coal.

From being a penniless refugee herself fleeing Hitler's
Germany, she had become a voice for the displaced people
of Europe. Her present award was justly deserved. It left
him feeling humble and inadequate. He raised his eyes from
the newspaper and looked around the gravy-coloured room.
Two older men sitting in silence by the pot plants in the
window bay quickly dropped their eyes. He had obviously
been the object of their scrutiny. Was he going to continue
to sit here, he asked himself, in this god-forsaken place and
turn into one of these? Was this the best he could do?

A new resolution inspired by Hilde's example was form-
ing inside his head. If he could do nothing for himself then
he could do something for other people. Unwittingly Hilde
had shown him a way forward.

He got to his feet and tucked the paper under his arm. 'A
Happy New Year to you,' he addressed the two men briskly.
'Maybe you'd like a seat by the fire.'

One lifted a critical eye. 'Aye. Maybe we would.' But

146

they waited until he had left the room before they picked up their whiskies and took his place by the fire. The mistress of the house would settle their curiosity when she came in to inspect the coal scuttle.

Back in his room he read the citation in the newspaper once more, then sat down to write a letter to his bank. When, after a few days, a reply came he went out to do shopping for some essential additions to his wardrobe. Then he settled his hotel bill and booked a seat on a train to Eastport, changing at Edinburgh.

Eighteen

The taxi he hired at Eastport Station put Andrew down at numbers 22–24 Percy Crescent, an impressive sweep of solidly built, three-storey houses. The attics and basements would have been servant accommodation in Victorian times. Now most of the houses were converted into smart flats except numbers 22 and 24 which were combined to make another Mullerman Sanctuary. The large sign at the end of the drive stated:

REFUGEES OF ALL NATIONS, THE HOME-LESS AND THE PERSECUTED WILL FIND SANCTUARY HERE.

PROPRIETRESS H. MULLERMAN SRN SCM

– and the paint was not yet dry on the **DBE.**

After reading this, Andrew knew, without a shadow of doubt, that he had done the right thing by coming here. If she would have him, he would work for her. He wanted nothing more than to be allowed to work with her for a cause in which he, too, sincerely believed. He walked up the short drive and pushed open the glass-fronted door.

The first thing he noticed as he entered the hall was the fresh sweet air – no drenching disinfectant but a shining cleanliness proclaimed itself. Trust a German, he thought ruefully. The interior was impressive, as one would expect in the house of a well-to-do gentleman of the previous century. High ceilings with moulded cornices, well proportioned windows, gleaming parquet floors. There were flowers everywhere. Where on earth did she find the money to run a place like this?

'Good morning.' A young lady was eyeing him from a reception desk. 'Can I help you?'

By design Andrew had sent no warning of his visit in case Hilde discouraged him. 'Is Miss Mullerman – Dame Hilde, available? I am an old friend.'

'Your name please.'

'Dr Andrew Mount.'

There was some telephoned conversation during which Andrew was waved to a chair. Eventually, of course, Hilde agreed to see him. She had very little alternative when he was there in person. The last time they met was at Cathy's wedding just after the war, twenty-five years earlier.

For a long moment they faced each other in solemn silence. The receptionist, indulging her curiosity with a quick squint, wondered about Dr Mount. Nice-looking chap. It was Hilde who spoke first. Andrew seemed lost for words. The slow sweet smile he remembered so well spread across her face. She put out her hand.

'My dear Andrew. Simon told me you were in Australia.'

'I've come back.' There were changes in her appearance, of course, as there were in himself. He knew her age. She was three years younger than he. That made her fifty-one. Her raven-black hair was brushed with a wing of startling white at the temples like the flash of a magpie. The business-like skirt and jumper she wore made no concessions to a thickening waist. All this was unimportant to Andrew. Had she been wizened, toothless and bald she would still be the woman he loved.

He found his voice. 'I hope this is not inconvenient. I

149

didn't let you know in advance in case you said I must not come.' He smiled his boyish, vulnerable smile and she laughed.

'Cunning Doctor Mount, you know me too well and you were right. I would have said, "No, you cannot come because I am too busy to see you." But now you are here, I am glad.' She turned to the girl at the desk. 'Ask Winifred to bring coffee, please.' The quick glance at her watch, however, did not escape Andrew's notice as he followed her into her office.

Coffee made an immediate appearance and they launched into the kind of enquiries expected between two friends after a long absence, Andrew was pleasantly surprised to learn that Hilde, the loner, had kept in touch with several of their old friends.

'Eric keeps my accounts in order. Evie and her Gladstone take my old people for drives in the country and one of their sons brings his pop group to sing for them. Simon is splendid. He begs lots of money from his rich friends and has provided a modern operating theatre here for minor surgery.'

'Good for him. I'm about to contact the old rogue. How is he?'

She smiled. 'He is just Simon. As always.'

Andrew took a deep breath. Time to talk. 'I must tell you what has brought me here, Hilde.' He saw, but ignored, the wary look that appeared in her eyes. 'I admire what you are doing. Your award is well deserved and I congratulate you.' She began to fidget. 'I am at a loose end and I have come to ask if you would consider taking me on your staff.'

She stopped fidgeting and her eyes opened wide in surprise.

Andrew continued, 'I want no payment. I want to help.' He hurried on as she was about to speak 'You may remember that I was a prisoner myself for five years and have some sympathy for others who suffered under much worse conditions. I am serious, Hilde. Please do not turn me away.'

She pushed up her lips in an unattractive gesture of discouragement. 'You are surprising me. Our work here is not to be undertaken lightly. I will show you over the Sanctuary, Andrew. You will see what we do here. That will be the time to ask if you may join us.'

They walked through rooms where men and women of different ages were engaged in various handicrafts. Hilde greeted them by name and was rewarded in most cases by a smile. 'My residents like to help to raise money by making things for our annual sale.'

In an adjoining conservatory an elderly man was re-potting plants, setting seeds. To judge by his total absorption in his task it would seem that the therapy, if that is what it was, was working. Andrew followed Hilde into the rambling garden where drifts of early snowdrops lay under the bare trees. Solitary figures wrapped in donated greatcoats of ill-considered sizes walked, heedless of the sharp January wind, heads down as if in silent contemplation.

'Life has bent them,' said Hilde. 'They have forgotten the sky.'

In the vegetable garden Hilde introduced Andrew to Dave. 'Dave is Polish. He grows all our vegetables and keeps the garden looking nice.'

Dave had one good eye and an artificial leg. 'Dese sprouts is gettin' no bloody good, Miss Mullerman.' He spoke in an extraordinary blend of Polish and English with Geordie overtones.

'But the cabbages are wonderful!' Hilde encouraged him. 'Dave was in the Polish Air Force,' she explained to Andrew. 'When the Nazis invaded his country he escaped

151

to England and flew with the RAF at Cassino. There he was wounded.'

Andrew asked if he did not want to go back to Poland, 'now that the fighting is over?'

'I am Englishman now. Here in England I am free.' He spread his big workaday hands and waggled his head. 'Maybe if I go back to Poland I not so free.'

'Have you family there?'

His one good eye blazed beneath bushy eyebrows fixing Andrew with an angry glare. 'Germans come with tanks. Polish soldiers fight on horseback. Brave men all killed. Then Russians come to finish the job. My family –' he spread his hands, 'all gone.' He turned to Hilde with sudden affection, displaying broken, yellow teeth in a wide smile. 'Miss Mullerman my family now.'

Hilde smiled. 'Though I am German, too, but I try to make amends for my country.'

Dave grunted to be trapped like this. 'Good Polski, bad Polski. Good German, bad German. Miss Mullerman best German.'

Twenty-five years since the fighting came to an end, Andrew was thinking, and still there are people like Dave, washed up after the tide of war recedes, on any shore that offers to help. 'Dave seems to have found peace at last, poor chap,' he said.

She smiled up at him. 'Growing my "bloody sprouts". He *is* happy now. No more tries to kill himself.'

She led Andrew, last of all, to the bedridden and the dying. Two large rooms in the original house had been turned into a ward. The pale winter sunshine poured in through tall windows, alighting on bowls of flowers and on tidy beds that were scarcely disturbed by the wasted bodies of the occupants.

The scene took Andrew back to the hospital hut which was his responsibility in the POW camp. His POW patients, like these persecuted men who had no hope left, had drawn the wrong cards in the game of life. They were losers. But there were differences here. These men lay in snow-white sheets. Gentle women tended them. Such comforts were denied the sick prisoners in Andrew's camp hospital.

'Amnesty International brings these poor men to me,' Hilde was explaining, 'not only war. Evil men still torture prisoners and sometimes there is little we can do.'

Andrew, standing quietly at Hilde's side, was aware of an atmosphere of peace in this ward, the still calm before death brought its own release. He could find no words to express his admiration for the strength of purpose which enabled Hilde to endure and devote her life to easing the tragedy about her.

'I will take you to Joseph.' She led him to a man whose age was hard to guess, who made a feeble attempt to raise a stick-like arm in greeting when he saw her. She took his hand in hers. 'Joseph, here is Dr Mount who is coming to work for us.'

In this way Andrew learned that he was accepted.

'What happened to Joseph?' he asked as they moved away.

'Since eight years old he is in Auschwitz concentration camp with his mother and his grandmother. He must sort the clothes of people gone into the gas chamber. One day he sees there his mother's flowery blouse. When the liberating army comes they find an idiot boy.'

She turned her head at Andrew's silence. Reading his struggle to contain his emotion, she reached out to take him by the arm and lead him away. For the first time these two disparate characters found common ground in their agony over the disinherited, degraded and disabled of the twentieth century.

It was meant to be, Andrew told himself as he took his

153

leave later that day. For what better reason did I become a doctor?

'Supper's nearly ready,' said Mary. 'Has Reg not come in yet?' She left the stove, fumbling for her stick. 'He's late.'

Marian raised her eyes from a dish of potatoes to glance out of the kitchen window. 'It'll be dark soon.' A whiff of anxiety could be sensed in the air. 'What's keeping him?'

Lily, scrubbing pans at the sink, paused for a moment, 'Mister Reg long time sittin' on the verandah.'

Marian put down the potato masher in surprise. 'What the dickens is he doing out there?' Hastily she wiped her hands and went to investigate.

'Mister Reg not feeling well, Lily.' Marian's mother sank into a chair. 'I am a little worried about him.'

Lily had been with the family for so many years she was sensitive to any undercurrents of change, particularly in matters which upset Missus Dan now that she no more had her man to look after her. 'Mister Reg sad,' she agreed. 'Not happy any more.'

Marian came upon him slumped in one of the creaky old cane chairs on the verandah where dusk was already cloaking everyday objects in shadow. His eyes were closed, his face fallen in loose fleshy folds. In some alarm she took his hand, lying there on his lap, dirty, unwashed, limp. He opened his eyes and looked at her as if she were a stranger.

'Reg,' There was alarm in her voice. 'What's the matter? Are you ill?'

He made no answer but wrenched his hand away from her, turning his head to stare glumly over the darkening paddock.

Marian frowned. 'Tell me if you are not well then we

can help. If you are not ill then for God's sake tell me why you are sitting out here, grumpy as an old bear. Supper's ready and you haven't even cleaned yourself up yet.'

'Too right,' he turned to face her. 'I stink. That's what you think of me.'

Marian was silent for a long minute. The line of her jaw hardened. 'OK, chum. It's talk-time. I have put up with your moods for a long time. You have scarcely exchanged a civil word with me for weeks. I don't know what's biting you but you are going to tell me. If you are ill, I want to know.'

'What the hell do you care.'

'Reg! I am your wife.'

'Are you? And am I your husband?'

She straightened in astonishment. 'Would you mind explaining yourself.'

He was silent, morosely withdrawing from her presence.

'You are changed, Reg. You are not acting like the man I love.'

That triggered a furious response. He jumped to his feet, his lips blanched with anger as he towered above her. 'That's bloody good coming from you.'

There was violence in the air. Marian had never before seen him so roused to anger nor such a look of malevolence in his eyes. For a moment she felt a quiver of fear, instantly suppressed, for it was nonsense to be frightened of Reg. 'What the devil is eating you, man?'

He gave a short, hard laugh. 'What's eating me? Do you want to know why I feel like slashing my wrists? Because I know that my wife has been unfaithful. You are right when you say that I am not the man you love. That bloody English doctor has your love and there's not a damn thing I can do about it.'

There was a stunned moment as Marian took in what

he was saying, then she flew at him like a wild thing, beating his chest with both her fists. 'How dare you! How bloody dare you! Reg Reed, you will take that back.'

He grabbed her two arms and held them in a vice so she used her feet and her knees, her rage lending her strength. She kicked and kneed him, struggling with all her might against his superior strength. At last she was crying, exhausted by her anger. 'Reg, how can you say such a terrible thing to me.'

Now the sight of her in tears tore him apart. He had made her cry. His self-loathing was complete. The passion went out of him and, though he still had his arms about her, they had lost their violent intention.

'Marian. Don't cry. Marian.' Then, as she continued to weep with her face against his sweaty shirt, 'Don't cry, little love. Don't cry. You are breaking my heart.'

'How could you,' she sobbed. 'How could you think such a thing? Whatever have I done to deserve this? The English doctor you are talking about was our friend. Andrew and Norah, our friends, nothing more.'

'There, there.' As if she were a small child, he wiped her tears with his red checked handkerchief. 'I watched you being nice to him, going off on rides with him. I thought I'd lost you, Marian.'

She pulled herself away from him. 'What has happened to trust, Reg? Isn't there supposed to be trust between man and wife?' She felt drained and empty.

He stood before her in pitiable contrition. 'Try to forgive your oaf of a husband. You are the most precious thing in my life, Marian. I think I lost my reason when I thought that Andrew was about to steal you.'

The sound of Mary's stick tap-tapping over the parquet floor brought them both back to reality. 'Marian!' her mother was calling, 'Is everything all right?'

Marian reached to take Reg's woebegone face in her hands and kissed him. 'Everything is all right, Mother,' she called over her shoulder. 'Reg had dozed off. We're coming now.'

She took Reg's hand, his little lover, his little mother. 'Come on, get cleaned up. Supper will be ruined.'

Nineteen

Every morning Norah was the first to pick up the post from Cathy's doormat and every morning she was disappointed. Cathy would look up from her prunes and yoghurt. 'Nothing from Andrew?'

'I'm getting really worried, Cat. Where can he have got to? He's had time to sail twice round the world since I left him in Sydney.'

'Perhaps he's still in Australia. Perhaps he wasn't able to get a passage.'

'He could have written.'

He did, at last. One fine morning in May. Norah hurried into the kitchen to share it with Cathy. 'Funny thing! It's got an Eastport postmark.'

'Oh, do get on and open it, Auntie Norah,' urged Alison. 'Are you going to read it or frame it!'

Andrew was a great favourite with Cathy's children. His godson, Philip, was mid-term at Bristol university. Michael and Alison, getting ready to go to work and school respectively, were eagerly waiting to hear the latest news of him.

Norah scanned the first few lines. 'You're not going to believe this.'

'Try me,' Cathy suggested.

'He's working for Hilde at the Jesworth Sanctuary.'

Cathy's toast was halted halfway to her mouth. 'How on earth did that come about?'

158

Norah referred to the letter:

It's time I made myself useful and I can't think of anywhere more rewarding than here amongst Hilde's lost souls.

Alison looked up from packing her schoolbag. 'I'd like to help Auntie Hilde as well, Mum. I think I'll be a doctor or a nurse, instead of an actress.'

'You'll always be an actress, dear,' Norah said with a tight smile. 'Whether you are a doctor or whatever.'

Alison ignored the little dig. 'Is he coming to see us?'

'Doesn't say but he will, for sure. He didn't come by sea after all,' Norah continued. 'He got a lift on a plane going to Scotland. *"I have a story to tell next time I see you"* he says.'

'I'll bet!' Michael got up from the table. He was a hefty lad of eighteen, very like his mother in colouring while Alison, lean and lithe, had a deceptively fragile look inherited from her father though she was actually as tough as either of her brothers when 'push' came to 'shove'.

'He'd better come soon before he forgets about us entirely.'

When they had both gone, Michael to catch the train to Leytonstone and Alison for the school bus, Cathy and Norah perused the letter for every last bit of information that might throw light on this unexpected development.

'He'll not get fat on Hilde's payroll,' Cathy observed. 'She spends every penny raised by charity on her residents. Every time I go to see her she seems to wear the same old threadbare jumper and skirt. I think she lives on rice pudding and potatoes.'

Norah went back to the letter. 'He's got an Ear, Nose and Throat consultancy at the Eastport General.' She smiled at

159

Cathy. 'Our old stamping ground. He says it buys his socks and his whisky.'

'Events have come full circle. Isn't it astonishing, Norah? Andrew is now as near to Hilde as he will ever get. If this were a romantic novel, he would win her love at the end and make her his wife.'

'But it isn't and he won't.'

In order to give Cathy more private time with her family – and especially with prickly Alison – Norah decided to look for a job. She was snapped up almost immediately to act as receptionist to an elderly doctor in the vicinity who had no time for young flibberty-gibbets. A woman of Norah's age and experience suited him very nicely.

Once she was earning again, Norah went a little further and wondered if Cathy would mind very much if she looked for a place of her own, a little flat, not too expensive.

Cathy's reaction was predictably accommodating. 'Of course not, Norah dear. As long as it's not too far away.'

It was, by common consent, a sensible plan.

'Because we've each got our funny little ways.'

'And they're likely to get funnier as time goes by.'

Together they visited estate agents in the area, haggling for an acceptable price as they had learned to do in the markets of Cairo years ago. Financial help came at a propitious moment from an unexpected quarter. Reg, who regularly forwarded to Norah the rent paid by the tenants of her little house in Dog Creek, now wrote to say he had a prospective buyer.

'Listen to this, Cat.' She read from the opened letter in her hand. 'The assistant doctor in Dog Creek wants to buy my house. It's handy for the clinic and, gosh, he's offering hundreds of dollars! He's recently married and intends to build on a nursery and another bathroom and goodness

knows what. Can you imagine? My little humpy is going
to make me rich!'

'Just at the right time,' said Cathy. 'You can raise your
sights a bit in choosing your flat.'

'Dog Creek is booming according to Reg. Good sheep
country, of course and the price of land keeps going up. I'll
write straight away and tell him to sell. And there's more
good news. He and Marian are planning to visit us. Maybe
next year. They've taken on an extra hand to help with the
stock since Dan died and they will be able to leave him in
charge.' Excitedly Norah hugged Cathy, 'You and Marian
will be able to meet. What I've always hoped for.'

Cathy nodded enthusiastically. 'We'll have a party.'

'Reg specially asked for Andrew's address. He intends to
look him up right away.'

'There's a good train service to Jesworth.'

The search for a home for Norah was renewed with added
zest and produced a very suitable ground-floor flat across
the Green from Cathy's house. It was part of a substantial
Victorian house and had two good-sized rooms, a modern
bathroom and kitchen, and the luxury of central heating.
Norah moved in and found that her windfall would stretch
to a small car.

'We can go for picnics.'

'Theatre? Shopping?'

'Anything you like, Catypus.'

'When did you learn to drive?' Cathy had never mastered
that skill.

'I used to drive Reg's tractors and Dr Jebb's old jalopy
when he overdid the whisky.'

Alison, for the very first time, was impressed by Auntie
Norah.

Norah wrote to Andrew with the good news that Reg and
Marian were intending to visit England the following year.
He would be surprised. And a little uneasy.

In fact, when the meeting between himself and Reg came about it was painless. Andrew had no desire to see him, no wish to open that closed chapter in his life which had caused him so much pain, such anger, but Reg gave him no opportunity to avoid what, at best, would be a very embarrassing situation. His note stated simply that he was coming and he came.

He was alone. For that Andrew was thankful. Coolly and professionally he led Reg to his study in the Sanctuary. Andrew could find no warmth in himself.

Reg took over at that point. 'I'll not sit down. I may not be staying long. I am expecting you to throw me out. Before you do that I will say my piece and square my conscience once and for all. I have come to apologize, Andrew, for the way I acted, the things I said about you and Marian. I was driven out of my senses by jealousy and I know now it was unfounded. I have caused you and also Marian a great deal of pain. Whether you accept my apology is up to you but I am telling you now, and I mean it, I have never in my life regretted anything so much as the things I said. There. I have done what I can to mend the damage. I'll go. Maybe as time goes by you will be able to think not too hardly of me.'

Andrew's planned cool approach was undone in a trice. Only to look at Reg, a former friend with whom he had shared so many good times in Australia, standing before him, wretched with shame, dissolved all his resolutions. Impulsively he thrust out his hand. 'It is forgotten, Reg. We will put it behind us and start again.'

Reg's troubled face was transformed by a huge beam of relief. Gladly he took Andrew's hand, pumping it up and down in gratitude.

'Hang on. I need that hand again,' Andrew laughed. 'I'd forgotten you've got the strength of a bull. Come on now, sit down. Tell me all about Wirrawee. I'll ring for some coffee – or tea? Which?' He picked up the phone.

After that, it was easy. Andrew took Reg over the Sanctuary, to show him the good work that was being carried out, then drove him to his train. A week later he drove south for Cathy's party, a great occasion where old friendships bloomed again and Cathy joined in.

Arriving back in Wirrawee, Reg inhaled a great breath of wattle and gum, of cows and sheep, manure and gardenia, and Lily's baking. A horse neighed. 'That's Moonbeam!' Marian cried in delight. 'He knows I'm home.'

Without preamble Reg stooped and lifted her off her feet and carried her over the threshold. 'So do I.'

Reg was not the kind of bloke to bother with photo albums, but he did have a sturdy morocco-bound volume where the big events of his life were portrayed, certificates of merit for his prime beef cattle won at Sydney Easter Show, awards for woodmanship and tree felling, a wedding photo. He wasn't so fat then.

There had been no new entries for some time but he was about to make one now. He carefully unfolded a letter.

> Dear Mr Reed,
> On behalf of all the residents of the Jesworth Sanctuary I want to thank you for your generous cheque. This has enabled us to install the very latest equipment to help our handicapped patients in and out of the baths. For them it is an immeasurable boon.

The letter was signed, *Hilde Mullerman DBE Proprietress.*

If the signature had been that of the Queen of England it could not have meant more to Reg.

Part Three

Twenty

FRIDAY 18 AUGUST 1995. This was the eve of the fiftieth anniversary of VJ Day, the end of the Second World War; something to celebrate, a glorious end to an inglorious conflict.

From the north, south, east and west of the country people were pouring into London to join in the celebrations; to honour the veterans who would be parading and to remember the thousands who gave their lives in the cause of freedom.

The capital was *en fête*, sedate London buildings in party mode. Against a sky of cloudless blue, Union Jacks flirted with the wispy summer breezes above the smart shops in Piccadilly, Oxford Street, Regent Street and the rest. Miles of bunting linked lamp post to lamp post and there were flowers everywhere, in hanging baskets and window boxes, red geraniums, white alyssum and blue lobelia.

Celebrations were not restricted to London. Village committees throughout the land had long been making plans for this day, organizing street parties, praying for fine weather, and now it seemed that their prayers would be answered. There had been no rain for five weeks. Temperatures had remained in the 30s and there were no signs of change.

At the Jesworth Mullerman Sanctuary preparations for the residents' party on the following day were going ahead. Cathy's daughter, Dr Alison Poole, had taken over the post of medical superintendent in that renowned institution upon Andrew's retirement ten years earlier. She was now the principal in all but name. The Dame's wishes in respect of the running of the Sanctuary were always strictly adhered to but their execution was left to Alison. Hilde was becoming increasingly frail through self-neglect, putting the welfare of her charges before her own.

She was not inclined to attend the Queen's victory parade in London until her friends persuaded her that, this being in her case a personal invitation from the Queen herself, she would be expected to accept if it were at all possible. Andrew clinched the matter by offering to drive her to London where she would join Cathy and Norah and attend the events in their company.

She was in her room at the Sanctuary this morning, preparing for the journey, while Alison and the senior sister of the home, Helen Beamish, checked arrangements for the next day.

'Carricks Cakeshop has turned up trumps.' Helen's pleasant, open face reflected her enthusiasm. 'They have stipulated "no fee" for their service.'

'That's very generous of them. The Dame will be pleased.' Alison was balanced gracefully on a corner of the sister's desk, coffee cup in hand, one long trouser-clad leg swinging casually above the parquet floor. Anyone who had known Ray Webster, Alison's father, would have recognized certain characteristics in his daughter, as in her easy, seemingly lighthearted manner which concealed an unsuspected touch of iron. Tall and slim as he had been, she moved with grace. She had the same long oval face and tousled blonde hair, and, when necessary, the same slightly amused way of deflating pomposity.

'And I have six volunteers from the public to help serve the teas,' Helen Beamish continued.

'I will be here all day,' Alison reminded her, 'and Julian will be here to look after the band and the entertainer.'

'It will be a family party for the residents as the Dame wishes.'

'She could call off the trip to London if she thought her beloved family was missing out on the celebrations.' Alison looked at her watch. 'Is someone helping her to dress?'

'Eva is with her now.'

'The little deaf one from Romania?'

'Madame is very fond of her, poor little thing. Incidentally, Alison, your mother chose a wonderful outfit for the Dame. At first she said she could not possibly go as she had nothing to wear but your mother carted her off to Fenwicks, explained the nature of the occasion to a smart sales woman and the trip was on. Wait till you see her. She looks exactly the way a Dame should look.'

Alison smiled. 'When my mother gets the bit between her teeth there's no stopping her. They are very old friends, you know. Did you know? During the war Dame Hilde was a refugee from Nazi Germany. She came to train as a nurse at the same hospital as my mother and Aunt Norah. She was wretchedly unhappy at first. Norah and my mum befriended her and they have been buddies ever since.'

'And she's made it her aim in life to look after other refugees no matter where they come from.' The sister consulted the wall clock. 'Dr Mount should be here soon. It will be a long, hot drive for both of them.'

'Her dear Andrew will look after her.'

'Was there a romance there? Not that it is any of my business. He seems very fond of her.'

'Hilde was never the marrying type, according to my mother. Anything that got in the way of her crusade to help the helpless was ditched. But she and Andrew have always been close friends.'

'They must have been fun to know, that little circle of friends before the war. I bet your mother and Norah were real smashers and I've seen pictures of the Dame where she

169

looks like a film star. As for the dear old Brig, I could go a bundle over him even now.' Helen peeped coquettishly at Alison. 'Your father in law, I'm talking about.'

Alison laughed. 'Hairy old trooper. But I agree, he has a certain old-fashioned charm. They say – who says? I'll rephrase that. It is said that he carried a torch for my mum for years and years and then she married someone else.'

'So you might have been the Brig's daughter.'

'No. Never that. I am my father's daughter.'

To break the touch of solemnity induced by Alison's unassailable statement, the sister pointed to the date circled in red on the desk calendar. 'Do you think the date and the name "VE Day" mean anything to our residents?'

'To some of them. The older ones. Talk to Dave about Poland. Some have been remembering, things they wanted to forget at one time. Now, suddenly, they want to talk about their often terrible experiences. That can only be good for them.'

'Unless it makes them depressed.'

'They're not depressed. They feel safe here, with us, and they are ready to have some fun tomorrow. The band will be popular. Music seems to get across to all of them, even Sven, the Misery Man.'

The sister laughed. 'He's in the conservatory blowing up balloons.'

'And bursting them.'

Footsteps sounded on the stairs. 'Whoops! Here she comes.' Alison slid from her perch and went to meet the figure who appeared at the head of the stairs, Dame Hilde Mullerman, holding on to the bannister rail for support but nevertheless making an impressive entrance. She was dressed in a silk dress and jacket of deep indigo relieved at the neck by a chiffon scarf of the palest pink. With her thick plaited hair of startling white against an olive skin, her huge dark eyes which Cathy long ago had likened to black olives, her obvious frailty became intriguingly attractive. She smiled nervously at Alison.

'Will I do?'

Norah and Cathy were on their way from Liverpool Street Station in London to the hotel where they would spend the night. Norah pressed her face to the taxi window as they were driven through Mayfair. 'There was another Piccadilly, Cat. Remember? Tarpaulin covering holes in the roofs, windows boarded up. Just look at it now.'

Splendid buildings. Smart shops. Choice displays of merchandise and people, men, women and children, like a stream of orderly ants going about their business in determined progression, like a river in flood.

Just released from the trains into the heart of London, families were making for their night's lodgings in preparation for the celebrations of the next day. Veterans searched faces of a likely age for old mates. In many a wallet a faded snapshot was a cherished reminder. An old mate could turn up and you never forgot an old mate. Maybe some of the old gang would march in tomorrow's parade, falling in behind their association banner, their blazers bright with medals.

Among the women veterans were those who once wore the tight little skirts of the ATS, the WAAF or the WRNS. They stood clutching their big handbags at the edge of the pavement, signalling for taxis, longing to sit down.

There were grandmas who remembered dried egg and good neighbours and jokes about the shelters, and there were subdued long-term widows with dimming memories.

London was steaming. Heat pressed down from a vaporous sky. Cathy dabbed her face with a handkerchief. 'This cab is like an oven.'

'We'll be there soon. The Warrington will be airconditioned.' Norah showed no sign of being overcome by the heat. Her straw hat sat tidily over the neat bun at her neck. Her naturally pale cheeks were only slightly pink.

'It's all right for you,' Cathy cast a crabby look at her friend. It was a well-known fact that thin people didn't feel the heat so much as well-covered types. 'You got used to this kind of heat in Australia. I'm sweltering.'

'This is not like Australian heat,' Norah protested. 'No "southerly buster" to blow it away. I think even Marian and Reg will find this hard to bear.'

'Where are they staying?'

'The usual. Strand Palace. We'll see them tonight. It's sad to think that this visit may be their last. Reg has not been well since his transplant.'

'Marian OK?'

'She's tough.'

Cathy tried to ease her shoe off a painful bunion. 'Thank the Lord we're not marching tomorrow. My feet are killing me.'

'The Warrington, ladies,' the driver announced. 'Your hotel.' Cathy and Norah began the usual squabble about who pays while their luggage was unloaded.

The Warrington was not as expensive as some West End hotels and had easy access to Birdcage Walk where the parade would muster the following morning. The interior was reassuringly old-fashioned. Nothing here to frighten old ladies. Cathy smiled her comfy smile as she glimpsed easy chairs and a bar. 'We can have a G and T in there,' she said 'while we're waiting for the others to join us.'

The hall porter stepped in smartly. 'This way, ladies.' He wasn't going to have them sloping off to the bar before he'd got them to their room. 'Here's the lift.' He was a youth of about nineteen years suffering from acne, but smartly turned out.

'Except for his shoes,' said Norah. 'He hasn't cleaned his shoes.'

172

He had been dealing with geriatrics since first light. 'Don't let me hear you calling them that,' his boss had said. 'They're veterans and you'll show them some respect.'

A couple of lively old girls, these two, he decided, as he bundled them out of the lift on to the second-floor landing. Groggy on their pins, though, and their tip was a bit old-fashioned but, like his boss said, they deserved some respect. He had a go at conversation. 'What were you doing in the war, ladies?'

'Nurses,' they said.

Might have known. They'd have you into bed with a tube up your backside sooner than you could say Jack Robinson. Need new specs, the pair of them. Couldn't even see the number on their door. He hoped their eyesight was better when they were cutting off legs and things in the war.

Lorna Poole was in the garden cutting flowers for the house when the silver Volvo belonging to her son Justin turned into the driveway.

'I'm in the garden,' she called out, and pulled off her gardening gloves. 'We need rain. The roses are wilting.'

'Just let it wait till after tomorrow.' He stooped to give his mother a kiss. She was quite tall but he was taller.

A small boy rushed up for his hug. 'Shall I get the hose out, Grandma?'

'Later, Max dear. After the sun goes down. It would only bake the ground now.' Lorna's usually cool appearance was awry, her cheeks flushed and damp strands of silvery hair straggled from under her wide straw hat. 'Come inside. I expect you'd like a nice cool lemonade.'

'Or a Coke,' her grandson suggested hopefully.

At forty-two Justin had the carriage of a soldier, created and refined on many a parade ground. He followed his mother and his son into the house.

Gabled and porticoed and discreetly screened behind

larches at the end of a drive adorned with camellia bushes, this was indeed, in real estate terms, a 'desirable residence'. The interior was equally impressive, proclaiming the loving care that was lavished upon it by a succession of 'little women' from the village.

'Did you get our tickets, Justin?' Lorna led the way to the drawing room, cool and shaded by half-drawn blinds.

Justin mixed a mint julep tinkling with ice for his mother and saw her comfortably settled before he went through the arrangements for the following day.

'Stand two.' He extracted tickets from his wallet. 'Numbered seats for Fiona, Max and yourself. I'll be on escort duty in the palace grounds but I'll detail a corporal to look after you. Be sure to wear a sun hat of some sort, Mother. There'll be no shade on the stands.'

'I suppose it would be anti-social to take a sunshade.'

'You'd be lynched,' her son agreed. 'Look out for the Websters. Philip and Michael will be there. Probably in the same stand as you.'

'And their mother, of course.'

'Cathy, Norah and Dame Hilde, as legitimate veterans, are all seated in the palace courtyard. They are not marching.'

'My grandad's marching, isn't he?'

'He certainly is, dear.'

'Will he be carrying a rifle, Grandma?'

'No, dear. An umbrella.'

This was puzzling but his grandmother was already discussing something else with his father. Max went in search of his friend, Poppy the cat.

'I thought Michael was in Australia mining copper?' Lorna was saying.

'This is a flying trip.'

'All this way? Just for the anniversary?'

'You are forgetting that his father was a captain in the Coldstream Guards. A crack regiment.' There was the tiniest hint of reproof in his voice. 'His sons and their mother will want to watch the parade even though, sadly, the father won't be taking part.'

Captain Justin Poole of the Royal Tank Regiment had seen no action and observed a healthy respect for those soldiers who had, especially the Guards of whom great feats were told. His own father had a war history scary enough to curl the hairs on the back of your head. He revered them all, originally young chaps who never intended to be soldiers, who were given a uniform and a rifle and told to get out there and kill Germans – survivors of this ill-starred generation, like his father and his friends, Dr Mount, ex-bank manager Eric Dotchin and Alec Cruddas, who had travelled from Canada for the occasion, who would be marching tomorrow.

'Where's Dad?'

'Gone for a hair cut. This will be his last parade, he keeps telling me. He's spent all day polishing his medals.'

'Can I see them, Grandma?'

'You must ask him yourself, dear. He should be here very soon. Put the cat down, there's a good chap. She's going to have kittens. Not just at the moment,' she added at his look of alarm, 'but soon.'

'It's going to be tough on him, marching in this heat.' Justin voiced his concern. He knew that his warrior father would never own up to weakness of any kind but he was now seventy-eight years old and there had been mention recently of unacceptably high blood pressure.

'Nothing will keep him from this parade.' His mother sighed. 'You know that.'

'Then make sure he takes his hip flask with him but filled with water not whisky.'

'Such a pity that Julian won't be there to see his father doing his "Eyes Left" at the Palace.' This was a little grudge that needed airing.

'Someone had to give Alison a hand with the residents' party at the Sanctuary and who better than Julian? He knows them all. Gets on well with them. He's booked a military band and entertainers. Without Alison and Julian to run the show the Dame would never have consented to leave her beloved "family", not even for an occasion like this.'

'I must say, I was surprised to learn she was coming to London. She has hardly set a foot outside the home for years. How is she getting here?'

'Andrew is driving her. She will be staying at the Warrington with Cathy and Norah.'

At the sound of an approaching car Justin went to the window. 'Here's Grandad now, Max. Off you go. Open the door for him.'

Simon began his booming as soon as he opened the front door. 'Hullo! Hullo! Hullo there! Who's been sitting in MY chair? Max, you scamp, what devilment have you been up to?' Holding his chattering grandson by the hand, he joined the others in the drawing room. 'I need a long, cold beer.'

'On its way.' Justin moved to get one. 'Getting in shape for tomorrow, Dad?'

Simon took a large handkerchief from his pocket and wiped his brow. 'Lord help us if it is as hot as this.' He pulled up a chair near his wife. 'All right, my dear?' He checked the climate with a quick diagnostic glance from under his wildly uncoordinated eyebrows and found her well disposed.

'We're all coming to watch you, Grandad.'

'Then I'll have to put my best foot forward, won't I.'

Max bent to study Simon's large splayed feet. 'Which is the best one?'

'Neither of them much good nowadays, lad.'

'Your grandfather was a first-class rugby player when he was a young man, Max,' said Lorna.

176

'Long time ago.' Ruefully, Simon stroked his flowing white moustache. 'Long, long time ago. Where's Fiona, Justin?'

'Making cakes for the local street party.'

'Good girl.' He turned to his grandson seated crosslegged at his feet. 'So, Mister Max, what is your programme for tomorrow.'

'Dad has got seats for Mum, Grandma and me in one of the stands and we're taking a picnic basket.'

'Excellent.' More seriously, Simon turned to his son. 'The girls fixed up, OK?' The 'girls' he spoke of, Cathy, Norah and Hilde, were all three in their late seventies.

'I booked them in at the Warrington. They have tickets and instructions for tomorrow. I'll get them to their seats in good time.'

'Good man.' Simon nodded and turned to his wife. 'I'll need to spend tonight in town, dear.'

'At the Army and Navy?'

'That's right. Four of us. Andrew, Eric, Alec and me. You haven't met Alec. Lives in Canada now. Ex-RAF. Battle of Britain pilot. One of Sir Harold Gillies's plastic surgery miracles.'

Lorna studied her immaculate nails. 'I will probably collect Paula this evening and do a theatre in town and a nice little dinner at Toni's.' Her price.

'Jolly good idea. See you tomorrow at the club after the parade.' Simon got to his feet, still a big, upright man, with a powerful chest and straight back. 'I'll take a shower then I'll get on my way. Got to check that Hilde and Andrew have arrived OK.'

'Max wants to see your medals, Dad.'

'Then come upstairs with me now, mister. Five minutes. Then I have to pack my gear.' He turned to Justin. 'Who's taking your mother tomorrow?'

'Fiona is coming to pick her up at 0930 hours. Corporal

177

Dennison is detailed to look after them for the rest of the day.'

'Is that all right with you, my dear?' On the slight nod from his wife, he grabbed his grandson by the ear. 'Come on then, if you want to see some medals.'

'I don't think you will need an umbrella tomorrow, Grandad,' Max confided as they went upstairs together. 'I don't think it's going to rain.'

After a cold lunch at the Warrington Cathy and Norah took themselves off for a walk in Green Park. Londoners were rejoicing in the very un-English temperatures and sunbathing as if on holiday in the south of France. Norah and Cathy loitered pleasantly in the coolness under the trees. They walked slowly, as old ladies do, stopping frequently to watch the children, and the swans dipping and preening on the pond.

'"Oh to be in England,"' Cathy quoted. 'Who said that?'

Cathy had imagined that she would feel sad at this time of remembrance when Ray was not there to share it. Instead she found herself warming to the good fellow-ship in evidence everywhere and the excitement here in the capital.

'Robert Browning,' said Norah, 'but he was talking about England in April.'

'I'm talking about this marvellous reunion of all kinds of people who have come to London to celebrate VJ Day. Fifty years later.'

'It's something special. People smile and greet each other in the streets.'

'And help old ladies up the steps.'

'You should be ashamed of yourself. You stand there, looking helpless, until someone comes to help. Usually a nice young man.'

'Young men like to help dotty old girls like me. It makes them feel like Boy Scouts.' She paused. 'Norah –'

'What?'

Cathy turned from the lake where children were sailing their boats to meet Norah's short-sighted glance. 'Do you ever think of Quentin, Norah? And Colin?'

Norah looked away. 'And Jackie. Of course I do. We must never forget them.'

'They were so unlucky.'

'And so brave.'

Cathy consulted her watch. 'We should be getting back to the hotel. Hilde and Andrew could be arriving at any time now.'

'And Marian and Reg.'

'Later.'

Simon was already there in the lounge. He put down the newspaper. 'I'll order tea. I've been waiting for you. Where've you been? You should be wearing a hat, Cathy, love. It's a powerful sun.'

'It would squash my hair. I've just paid a fortune to have it done.'

'We're all having dinner here tonight? Is that the drill?'

Cathy nodded.

'Have you ordered a table?'

'Course I have,' Cathy sparked. 'I'm not dotty yet.'

'Here comes the tea.' Norah made room for the tray amongst the spread of Simon's newspaper.

At that moment, the hall porter, the spotty one, held back the entrance door to admit Andrew and Hilde.

'Mrs Webster and Mrs Collins are in the lounge,' he said, 'with a visitor,' and this one, he told himself, looking at Hilde, is groggier than the rest of them. If that guy took his arm away, she'd fall down.

Hilde was pale but composed, smiling serenely as Andrew led her into the lounge.

Cathy and Norah were temporarily at a loss for words. Norah was thinking, 'She looks wonderful in that outfit' but Cathy could not take her eyes off Andrew.

This dear old man. This dear friend of so many years. Only one word could describe the radiance that shone from his face as he came forward with his lady on his arm – happiness. Total happiness. It had been a long time coming to him but life would never get better than this.

Cathy went up to them and kissed them. 'My dears, you both look wonderful.'

Norah poured the tea.

'It's nothing to cry about, pet!' Simon saw Cathy hunting for a handkerchief and handed her one of his own.

With her face buried in his nice, well-ironed handkerchief she smelt the old familiar smell of Simon that brought a host of memories reaching back over the years to their youth.

'I'm not crying really,' she insisted. 'It's just such an enormous thought that we are together again in our old age. Don't argue, Simon. That is what it is. Tonight, in spite of all the things that might have happened to us and did happen to some of us, we have survived together. It's too big for me to think about.'

'Give her a cup of tea, someone. Dry up, old girl.'

Twenty-One

1 9 August 1995. This was the day and still no rain, nor had the sun ceased shining. The heat was unrelieved and the excitement in the heart of London was intense. 100,000 people lined the Mall alone, six rows deep, and every seat in the stands surrounding the Queen Victoria Memorial was occupied. Cathy's sons, Philip and Michael, were there, Simon's family in the adjacent stand.

As the morning advanced so did the temperature rise. Women wearing the coolest possible dresses and big, shady hats were feeling the heat. Using their white paper programmes as fans they created a disturbance amongst the crowds like a wave of agitated pigeons. Old men protected their bald pates from the burning sun with cunningly knotted handkerchiefs. A sweating multitude welcomed with gratitude the First-Aiders who arrived to distribute water from portable containers.

Those veterans who would be taking part in the march to Buckingham Palace were already mustering in Birdcage Walk, wearing their association berets and blazers, unfurling their banners, waiting for the 'off'.

Cathy, Norah and Hilde had a place inside the palace forecourt with other veterans who would not be joining the parade. Together, these three elderly women presented a creditable display of campaign medals and awards but Hilde's DBE outshone the rest. The Queen on her walkabout had stopped to exchange a word with her. Hilde looked stunning in the new outfit. Her eyes sparkled with excitement and Cathy, seeing Hilde so obviously enjoying every minute of this very British occasion, took some pride in the fact that, without her determined persuasion, the Dame would not have consented to travel this far.

A sudden fanfare of trumpets announced the start of the parade and a rolling burst of applause greeted the arrival of the Household Cavalry at the head of a long procession of wartime associations, each identified by its individual banner.

The Royal Navy, the Merchant Navy, the Marines, the Commandos; the men who escorted Atlantic convoys in cockleshell corvettes; men on the dreaded Murmansk run. Famous regiments, famous battles were brought to mind by marching men no longer young but with experiences undimmed by age.

Cathy's heart leapt to see, amongst the famed Guards' regiments represented here, the colours of the Coldstreams. Glancing across to the nearby stand to see if her sons had marked their father's old regiment, she intercepted their grave salute with a nod and felt the sweet solace of her children's understanding.

Spontaneous shouts from the crowd of 'Thank You!' caught the men of the 14th Army Association off guard. These men fought on in Burma when the war in the west was finished. 'The Forgotten Army' was what they bitterly called themselves but today they were being rewarded by the nation's thanks. Surprise and delight lit up their faces. No longer forgotten as the rolling cries of 'thank you' and outbursts of clapping followed their progress from the palace up the length of the Mall.

The Paras were there and the Long Range Desert Group; dignified turbanned Indians and nuggetty Ghurkas, four of them wearing Victoria Crosses; the RAF, the men who flew Spitfires and Hurricanes and Lancasters, survivors of countless dangerous missions by night and by day.

Within this group a smaller company marched, some in wheelchairs pushed by their companions. Their banner read 'The Battle of Britain 1940', survivors among the air crew who, at terrible cost to their young lives, put an end to Hitler's plans to invade Britain. Immortalized in a tribute by Winston Churchill as 'the Few', they sent Hitler's invincible Luftwaffe into the Channel.

Ex-Flying Officer Alec Cruddas, one of the Eastport group of friends before the war, was one of those marching today under that historic banner. He walked confidently by the side of his wartime companions. From this distance the patches and puckers on his replacement face were not visible nor his lashless eyes. In his youth he had been every Juliet's dream of Romeo. His part in the war had cost him his good looks but not his buoyant personality.

Next came the Commonwealth contingent. Norah's grip on Cathy's hand tightened as she caught her first sight of an Australian slouch hat. She had known a man like these long-legged, spare characters with their hard eyes and tanned faces, a long time ago. Stooped now, finely drawn, tough as leather. This is how Keith would have looked today if he had lived. His sister, Marian, was somewhere in the crowded Mall today. She would weep to see the Aussies marching by.

'Here come the Dunkirk veterans.' There was the hint of a quaver in Hilde's voice as she drew attention to the approaching company. 'Simon leading.' As a student nurse she had cared for many of the wounded who were fortunate enough to reach England after the disaster of Dunkirk. Simon was one of them.

The leaders of each association needed no uniform to prove they were leaders of men. The bowler hat, the rolled umbrella and, above all, their bearing were conclusive. For young Max Poole the mystery of the umbrella was solved.

Brigadier Simon Poole cut a heroic figure. He marched with absolute precision, straight-backed, head high, his right arm swinging to the beat of the band, his brave white moustache a focal point on a face that was crimson with heat.

'He is *magnificent*,' murmured Hilde.

The men he was leading had survived the first terrible defeat of the war and had lived to fight again, and again. Simon could have chosen to march with the El Alamein Association or the Monte Cassino or the British Army of the Rhine, having served in all those campaigns, but Dunkirk was first blooding for him and his friends. It was their first encounter with the real thing after playing at war in the Territorials. It was Simon's time of enlightenment when he learned to hate, to kill; when his sergeant-major, an excellent man and superb soldier, was blown to smithereens on a doomed bridge while attempting to rescue a mother and her children. Even today, fifty-five years after that event, he tasted bile in his mouth at the memory.

Andrew, ex-captain in the Royal Army Medical Corps, was right behind his old friend. Keeping time, keeping in step and, at the same time, opening a file in his memory which had long been closed; of his last days on the beach at Dunkirk, operating in a shell hole as time ran out for the wounded to be evacuated, finding Simon slumped in the sidecar of a French dispatch rider, with a deep mortar wound in his back, the race to get him on board the last hospital carrier to leave the burning harbour, seeing the ship pull away and run the gauntlet of shells as she made for England with his best friend on board.

Andrew did not see Simon again until he, himself, was released from the POW camp five years on. Now, a lifetime later, he was responding to Simon's 'Eyes Left' as they passed the podium where stood the Queen and her ministers. Two old men, still in perfect harmony.

Behind Andrew came Eric. Eric, the unaspiring bank clerk of long ago, left with a permanent limp from the injury he sustained when he retrieved his friend's body from the minefield at El Alamein. He wore the Military Medal as well as the Africa Star. Eric never intended to be a hero. It just happened naturally.

The crowd responded to the Dunkirk banner with a burst of applause. A younger generation was quick to show respect for a nation which never knew when it was beaten, which was almost destroyed after Dunkirk, which stood alone after the fall of France, and continued to fight on for another five years until the Nazis were defeated.

'And I am a German,' whispered Hilde, 'yet you give me your medal for heroes.'

When the last company had taken its place in front of the palace a deep, attentive silence fell. No marching feet. No hand clapping or children's cheers nor beat of regimental bands. Even the birds were silent. Then the clear notes of the Last Post played by a lone bugler rang out over a city steeped in memories and awe.

A single wartime plane, a Lancaster bomber, broke the silence as it flew low down the Mall from the Admiralty Arch. As it rose to soar over the palace it released its load, not of bombs this time but 500,000 scarlet poppy petals, making a blood-red cloud against the heavenly blue of the sky. Gently, softly and silently the petals drifted down, poignant symbols of lives lost, and settled on the heads of men and women, bishops and chaplains, visitors from overseas and on Queen Victoria's pretty little crown.

Long after the noise of the plane's engines had died away the people stood still, absorbing the majesty of a moment when Britain paid homage to the men and women who made Britain safe from invasion and the rule of a tyrant.

In Birdcage Walk the marchers were falling out, rolling up their banners, lighting up their cigarettes; old men, all of them, dying for a pee and a beer. The long hot day was over. They spoke little. One said, for all of them, 'Make no mistake. This is the last parade. Look at us.' The speaker had shrunk in stature since he marched past the Queen. His new hip was giving him hell. 'We're crumbling away, the lot of us.' Quietly the men dismissed and went their own way, but they would never forget this one splendid day when the companionship they had known in the war years had been briefly restored.

Norah took Andrew's hand in farewell. 'Let's meet again before too long.'

Simon bent to Cathy's ear, tickling the back of her neck with his whiskers. 'This has been a day of memories for all of us. Some good, some not so good in our lives, yours and mine.'

Cathy turned to look seriously into his kindly face. 'It is the end of the chapter, my dear old man.'

'The end of the book, my dear old lady, and, all things considered, not such a bad finish after all.'